Adella M. Lawton

When Vaudeville Came To Joplin

Cynthia S Gillard

Copyright © 2012 Cynthia S Gillard
All rights reserved.

ISBN: 1468119281
ISBN 13: 9781468119282

Library of Congress Control Number: 2011963377
CreateSpace, North Charleston, SC

Acknowledgements

*For our children and grandchildren with special thanks to
Barbara Hastings Schaefer, Dorothy Hastings Johnston,
Richard Hastings, Linda Johnston, and Anne Jacobson.*

~ IN LOVING MEMORY OF LARRY JOHNSTON

WHEN VAUDEVILLE CAME TO JOPLIN
Prologue

Children begin by loving their parents; after a time they judge them; rarely, if ever, do they forgive them.

~OSCAR WILDE (1854–1900)

We came from such different worlds. We were certainly on different journeys, with paths not likely to cross, but cross they did.

He told me that he once was a sailor who came to America on a cold, blue sky, January day in 1905 when he was barely eighteen. He closed his eyes as he recalled the feeling of the cool, crisp air and bright sun of America on his face. The Statue of Liberty was, as promised, a delight to lay eyes upon and much larger than he had ever dreamed. When his ship landed soon after at Ellis Island, he was not sure what to expect and feared that customs would send him back to England. It had been a long twelve-day journey from England, but he was determined to step into this world of promise and not look back.

As he waited to disembark the steamship, *New York*, he studied the passengers huddled in groups under wool blankets struggling to keep warm. This trip had certainly opened his eyes. He understood how lucky he was to have purchased a second-class fare because he heard at least fifty people were crowded into many small bunkers on the third-class deck below. He overheard a third-class passenger complaining of the smell from so many folks clustered together and the wretched tasting food.

His cold fingers felt through his coat for the tobacco pipe in his pocket as he thought of his father, wondering if he would ever be able to make it right with him. They were so different, he would insist, that it was a wonder he was raised by the man.

As for his mother and sisters, he hoped to have the chance to see them again. When he left Bristol, England, for the new country, he was sure he had broken his mother's heart. His father, however, didn't have a heart, or so Clifford thought. His father had expectations that Clifford could not meet. Clifford believed his father's expectations were intentionally impossible—graduate from school, work in the family business, court a girl, get married, and lead the mundane existence that he and Clifford's mother preferred. That was his father's definition of success. As a young man, Clifford struggled with those expectations and swore that he would give it a go, but he just did not fit in that world. He would always tell me that "it was a damned wretched situation that he found himself in."

John Priest's world, after all, was so properly British. For as long as he could remember, there were rigid rules, of which John Priest was the architect and the strict enforcer. Children having fun and just being children was not a priority in John Priest's life, and children having a voice and expressing their feelings was never permitted. Even when his father was away, the tension in the house remained thick with his unyielding presence. Clifford knew he wanted something different, something more adventurous and creative than his father chose to imagine, much less allow. Clifford wanted to travel and see the world, experience life, and not from behind a desk.

So he set out to break ties with his father, which didn't take long as it turned out. It all came about when his father caught him smoking a pipe and joking around with some of the blokes out the backdoor of John Priest's factory, where Clifford was working as a machinist. He was appalled to catch his son, not only smoking in public, but violating the company's well-established work rules and with the employees no less.

So in the end, it was John Priest's idea that Clifford leave the family home and business.

"Get out and do not come back until you are a man," John Priest commanded after his son's offense. Clifford could have gone to London to find his life, but he wanted more, so he scraped together his savings and caught the first steamship in Southampton bound for the United States leaving his home, family, friends, job, any future he might have had in England, and the only world he had ever known. Alone for the first time, he was determined to make his mark in America, knowing it would be tough.

"Failure be damned," Clifford would repeat to himself, trying to bolster himself for the long journey that lay ahead.

As he stood in line waiting for his turn to disembark, he noticed a group of young girls staring and pointing at him. The tall, slender, well-dressed young man with the derby hat instantly felt self-conscious. He fiddled with the buttons of his long, black wool overcoat and adjusted the burgundy scarf around his neck. The sun glanced golden off his brown, windblown hair that fell below his hat. He tried to appear deep in thought as the girls giggled, looked at him, and giggled again. He thought they were betting which of them would have the nerve to gain his attention. With the hope that his brother would soon join him in America, Clifford turned away and dreamed of Boston, his first destination.

People sometimes ask about what life was like on the plains of America for a young girl during the early years of the twentieth century. Many faces and events flood the memories of my childhood in Joplin, Missouri. Much of my life back then appears clearer today. Living in the past is so much easier now because life makes more sense. Painful memories have all but disappeared. Through all of my life though, there is only one memory that I truly and deeply cherish. It is the memory that I dream about at night, the one I take with me wherever I go.

1

*America is the only country that went from barbarism to
decadence without civilization in between.*
~Oscar Wilde (1854–1900)

Joplin was called "jack city" because of all the miners there trying to strike it rich. They mined zinc, or what the locals called "jack." Lead was also mined in Joplin after having been discovered in some farmer's field soon after the Civil War. The townsfolk were proud of the fact that Joplin contributed six million tons of lead, nearly one-third of the lead from four surrounding states. Lead was the primary mineral that prospectors sought before zinc was recognized as a valuable resource. Zinc was tossed in the dump as worthless until folks discovered that it had value, too. The first batch of zinc that shipped from Joplin in the late 1800s fetched a whopping five dollars a ton and made a lot of Joplin people rich.

Many families who owned the larger mines lived in nearby Webb City. They hired the folks from Joplin to work their mines or to work in their homes as servants. The story goes that John Webb discovered lead in his cornfield in 1873 and the next thing you know Webb City was born. Mines dotted the countryside of Jasper County, so it was not uncommon for people walking at night to fall to their deaths in an open mine. Mines were everywhere. Mining brought Joplin folks wealth and food for the table, and it didn't take much to prospect and get a mine of your own. All that you needed was a pick, a shovel, and a pair of good, strong hands.

The folks in Joplin tried hard to act civilized to one another. We had everything in our town that a civilized town should have: schools, theaters, restaurants, clubs, civic organizations, charities, and an abundance of churches. The *Joplin Daily News* and the *Joplin Daily Globe* reported on events of the town.

A large stone courthouse stood right in the middle of town. The townsfolk had fought hard to have it built in Joplin. The American flag and the flag of Missouri hung from a flagpole on its rooftop, the tallest one in town, at least until it burned to the ground in 1911.

The courthouse was supposed to bring justice to the people of Joplin. Even some forty years after the Civil War ended, life in Joplin and surrounding places was anything but just.

Men and boys alike worked alongside each other in the mines, and young girls toiled in the Joplin laundries. The hours were long and the conditions deplorable. A minimum age law was eventually passed by every state protecting young children from being worked to death or close to it. It took the passage of a law to do what was right, and then it took several years before the lawman felt it right to enforce the law. Folks needed to eat, so they put their kids to work to earn the food. No law was going stop them from that. You see, that is how it was back then; if people didn't agree with a law, they just paid no attention.

Where there were miners, there were saloons. Where there were saloons, there was gambling, whoring, and drinking. I didn't know much about the brothels in Joplin as a child, but I came to know something about the saloons because Papa owned one and I lived right upstairs.

Thankfully, other kids lived within walking distance of the saloon. When I was real young, we all walked to school together, at least before that one day. The older kids were charged with watching over the younger kids, along the way. In my group, there were five kids, including me, Sarah, and three boys. Sarah, the oldest of the group, was a real pretty girl and I was her pretend little sister. The two younger boys, John and James, were her brothers. Luke, the oldest boy, never talked much. While Luke kept to himself most of the time, John and James were mischievous like the "Peck's

Bad Boy" character in the newspapers. They were always wandering off getting into trouble and making us late for school.

Springtime in Joplin was the best time of year. The dogwoods were in bloom, and it was always pleasantly warm, not hot like in summer. I remember one particular spring day in April 1903. We were all walking home together from school, and it was sunny and warm like you'd expect it to be.

Sarah had come to my school to fetch me for the walk home. I had stayed later that day to work on the spring talent show in which I was pegged to sing in the little girls' choir.

"Come on, Della," Sarah said, grabbing my hand and leading me down the front steps of my school.

John, James, and Luke were with her, but they were twenty steps ahead of us, as usual. I could never keep up with those wild boys. It was a good thing that Sarah always walked with me, especially that afternoon.

As we walked, I noticed a large crowd of folks, many that I recognized.

"Geez, look at all those people over there!" John yelled to James as they ran across the street toward the crowd.

Sarah's grip on my hand tightened as she jerked me across the street behind her chasing John and James. Before we reached the other side of the road, my foot hit a hole in the road, and I stumbled and fell, almost landing in a stinky pile of horse dung.

"You boys get back here!" Sarah yelled, stopping long enough to pull me to my feet as the boys ran ahead.

"I'll go up there with them," Luke said passing us by as he broke into a run.

Then we were running to try to catch Luke, who had almost made it to the back of the crowd. As we got closer, the crowd grew larger turning into a big wall of people. Of course, all I could see were legs. The crowd seemed to move as a single being, all in the same direction. Luke and the boys disappeared into the crowd by the time we reached it. Sarah stopped for a moment to sum up the situation and see if we should chance it by going in after the boys.

"Oh, we got to go in there 'cause I have to get those boys home from school. You stay right with me, Adella Lawton," Sarah decided, grabbing my hand even tighter and dragging me through the crowd like a rag doll.

I started to giggle, thinking this game of trying to catch the boys was fun. It seemed a lot like the game we played in the corn at Halloween. I had never seen so many people in one place at one time.

Sarah and I were getting bumped around and elbowed a lot, but no one tried to stop us. Sarah just kept pulling my little self along. Then, I fell down and my knee scraped against the stones on the ground. My knee was bleeding, and it stung. Sarah pulled me up to my feet again and continued pushing through the crowd and dragging me behind her. She kept calling out for the boys, but some of the folks around us were yelling bad words real loud and throwing things at something beyond. One man was on top of another's shoulders ordering everyone to go home and stop this nonsense. I heard someone yell, "Get the murderer!" A murderer had to be something real bad, but at the time I wasn't sure what it was.

Even after we managed to break through the crowd, Sarah held tightly to my hand. We found ourselves at the corner of Second and Wall Avenue with the boys nowhere in sight. The crowd had formed a circle around that corner. I started to pull away from Sarah to make a beeline to some folks that I recognized so I could show them my bloody knee. I stopped cold when I saw the man, and I could tell by Sarah's face that she saw him, too. Everyone was looking at him. He was a big colored man in brown trousers and a brown shirt. I wondered how his shirt got so dirty and torn, why his face was all swollen and red, and why his lip was bleeding like my knee. But what I wondered most was why there were men dragging him by a rope tied around his neck, like a dog. The crowd was now chanting "murderer" so fiercely and loud that it hurt my ears. When the colored man was able to get his footing, he limped along on one leg. His arms were tied behind his back. As he looked in my direction, I saw the terror in the man's eyes. I looked at Sarah. Her eyes told me that something awful was happening, and this was not a fun game. Sarah covered her gaping mouth with one hand and looked over at me.

"Let's get outa here, Adella!" Sarah gasped, yanking me back into the crowd. The last thing I remember seeing was the rope around that man's neck getting tossed up over a pole at the corner of Second and Wall.

Sarah was sobbing so hard when we finally cleared the crowd, and I wondered if she'd been hurt. I was so frightened that I forgot about my bloody knee and the boys, whom we never did find that day.

"Whatever happens, Della, don't...don't you go tellin' your ma and pa about what we saw...saw in town, okay?" she choked between sobs.

"Why not?" I asked, not sure what it was that I was not supposed to see.

"I just, I just don't want to get the boys in trouble," she said, gaining some composure. "It'll be our secret. Promise me that, Della."

I sort of liked the idea of having a secret with Sarah, but I didn't fully comprehend what the secret was all about.

"What was wrong with that colored man? What were those people doing?" I pressed her.

"There was nothin' wrong, Della. You just forget what you saw, you hear?"

And I didn't say anything to my folks about that day. I kept my promise to Sarah, at least, for a while. That night Papa saw my scraped up knee but didn't ask about it, and I didn't offer an explanation.

Years later, I found out that Papa knew there was a lynching at the corner of Second and Wall Street, just like he knew that we kids had walked through the town when it was going on. I learned that the colored man, Thomas Gilyard, had been lynched right after Sarah and I turned away from the corner of Second and Wall. He was accused of killing a white policeman down at the Joplin rail yards. A white man, Sam Mitchell, was later arrested for lynching Gilyard, but it would be real hard to get a jury in Joplin to punish Sam Mitchell much for what he did. Papa knew that most the folks in town saw this lynching as justice even though it wasn't given out at the courthouse.

Joplin's anger did not stop with that lynching. It went on all night long. Angry townsfolk tried to chase all the colored people out of Joplin and burned down their homes. The Robinsons, a colored family, was chased out of Joplin that day, along with a hundred other colored families. They left one of their kin, Joe Robinson, behind in Papa's care. Papa didn't like what had happened to the colored folk of Joplin that day, so he gave Joe a place to sleep and a job in the saloon.

There were people that came to town to stop the chasing and burning. Others just came to watch all the people that came to town to stop the chasing and burning. Mayor Trigg decided to close the saloons until things settled down a bit.

From that day on, I was taken to and from school in a buggy and was no longer allowed to walk with the kids. For a while, I wasn't even allowed on the streets of Joplin alone.

In church, we learned about heaven and hell. I didn't realize it then, but I am pretty sure that I saw hell the day those folks lynched Thomas Gilyard. I was just six years old.

2

My papa, Michael J. Lawton, whom most folks just called "Mike," was a tall, Irish man who wore round, wire spectacles that made him look more distinguished than he actually was. He always dressed in dark trousers, a white shirt, and suspenders, unless he wore his Sunday suit. When he was pondering something, he smoked his pipe. Of course, I never knew what he was pondering, but it must have been about the future because Papa did not know much about his past.

"My sister and I spent some time in an orphanage," he told me once. "But that ain't no excuse for not getting somewhere in life."

Papa's orphanage burned to the ground when he was quite young, and no shred of paper was left to identify any of the orphans who lived there. He had no birth records, but Margaret, his older sister, had a few more memories about their folks than my Papa had. She told him that their ma and pa came to America from Northern Ireland.

"Papa, where were you born?"

"Illinois," he would respond when we played the game.

"Where was I born, Papa?"

He would test me. "Idaho."

"No I wasn't, Papa."

"New Hampshire," he would tease.

"Papa…"

"You think you know…go on…tell me, young-in."

In Joplin, every kid was a *young-in'*.

"Louisiana, Missouri," I'd answer.

"Where do you live now?" he would test.

"Joplin."

"Do you know your address?"

"715 Joplin Street," I said with the conviction of a six-year-old, and he would nod in approval of my great wisdom.

Papa married Mama, whose name was Augusta Essenberg, when she was barely eighteen years old and he was about twenty-four years old. Mama's parents were German, and she was born in Pennsylvania. Her family made their way west to Missouri where they settled on a farm in Louisiana, Missouri. Papa met Mama in St. Louis, but they moved to Joplin because Papa wanted to own a saloon.

Aunt Margaret, whom we called "Maggie," and her husband, Sam Whittsett, came to live with us in Joplin. Having them in our home was like having an extra set of parents for me. I was forever the only child, and the ladies fussed over me like I was the only child in all of Missouri.

We lived above a saloon at 715 Joplin Street, and we had a large bay window in the front room where I could sit and watch the people on the street. The building had a cellar, where Mama stored potatoes, applejack, and home-canned goods. We also had a carriage house across the alley with a stable for the two horses that pulled our buggy and a small woodhouse to feed the wood-burning stove that kept us warm during the colder months.

Tall, slender, and dark haired, Mama, whom everyone called "Gussie," was a very attractive woman. Her hair was long, but she wore it in a knot at the back of her neck, in braids pinned up along each side of her head, or on special days she carefully piled it on the top of her head like the sophisti- cated ladies in the newspapers. Compared to me, Mama was a large woman, and she refused to wear a corset unless Papa was taking her someplace spe- cial. Mama preferred comfort to the fashionable hobble skirt of the time and loved to wear her broad-brimmed hats that fell just above her lovely brown eyes. Folks said I had crystal blue eyes like Papa and dark brown hair like Mama, but the truth was, I didn't favor either one of them.

Mama was a quiet religious woman, who worked hard to make our home a good one. Married women of her time did not have much control over their lives, at least not that they let anyone know. It was not acceptable then for a married woman to have a job outside of the home. Instead, they were expected to take care of the home, and raise up a house full of children. Mama and her housemaid cooked, cleaned, gardened, made, washed, and hot-pressed our clothes. She was in charge of running our household, but she didn't control the household money because that was Papa's job.

When I was a young girl, women didn't have the right to vote. And if Mama ever got the right to vote, she would likely vote the way Papa told her to vote. There were a lot of women, called *suffragettes*, speaking their minds about having voting rights. Out here in Joplin, even if Mama supported their cause, she probably would not have been a *suffragette*.

Mama appreciated the fact that she had running water and electric lights, which she did not have in her childhood home. No, where she came from there was a water pump and an outhouse. She still had a water pitcher and basin in her bedroom, and her bathtub was just that, a round tub. The light at night came from a kerosene lamp, if they could afford the kerosene. Papa always told the story about how Mama cried with joy when he bought her first electric lamp.

Mama may not have controlled the money, but she sure had a woman's wisdom in knowing how to go about getting what she wanted. She never complained about her life to me and of course, never to Papa. Instead, I think she just found ways to make it all work. She was forever thankful for what she had. Mama must have had her own dreams and aspirations, but it was expected that she would sacrifice her dreams for the good of her family. It was a sacrifice that Mama seemed more than willing to make.

I always knew that Mama wanted me to experience more in life than she'd experienced. I could tell by the way she acted and the little things she said, like how important it was for me to control my own destiny. "Independence and realizing your own potential is the path to true happiness," Mama would say. This was a novel idea for our time. Mama wanted me to have a different life, so she encouraged me to learn to do a lot of things on my own. She did not want me working in a saloon or cleaning rich folks' houses. Mama in her quiet way encouraged me to make something of myself and she insisted that I learn to play the piano.

Joplin had dances, concerts, county fairs, picnics, and church activities, but nothing compared to the fun that I experienced when Vaudeville came to Joplin. Mama and Aunt Maggie always took me to the Vaudeville shows in Joplin. I was drawn more to the music of Vaudeville than anything else. There was always a piano player at the theater who would play music during the shows. The piano was the most amazing instrument because it conveyed the full range of human emotion. Some songs made people laugh and others made them cry.

"Papa? When I grow up, I want to play the piano and sing songs and make people happy," I told him on more than one occasion. He would always just shake his head up and down, smile at me, and then go back to reading his newspaper.

On my eighth birthday, Papa brought home a small piano from Gottfried & McMillan's Music Store in Joplin. He placed it in a corner of the front room so that I had my own quiet place to practice. Papa had taken me seriously.

Once a week after that, I went to the Crockett's house to get my piano lesson. Mrs. Crockett directed the choir at the Grace Episcopal Church. Her girl, Olive, was my age and my best friend. Occasionally, Mrs. Crockett even had me play a hymn at church. It always made me smile with confidence when she called me her "child prodigy."

3

*I felt invincible. My strength was that of a giant. God was
certainly standing by me. I smashed five saloons with rocks
before I ever took a hatchet.*

~CARRIE NATION AKA CARRY A. NATION (1846-1911)

Papa made sure I went to church every Sunday. I think it was because he thought he was paying a debt to society by raising me right. After all, Papa owned a saloon in Joplin, a place where men escaped their family responsibilities, drank whiskey chewed tobacco and smoked the hemp weed to calm their nerves. Papa named it the Criterion Saloon. He used to tell people that he won the Criterion in a poker game. I don't know if it was true or if he was just telling tales because he loved to tell tales.

I was leery about liquor because I grew up with the lurid tale about the two boys and two girls, teenagers, who took liquor down to Joplin Creek and got exceedingly drunk. Their story made the news and became a shining example of what should not be done. The girls, who came from a brothel, were found passed out in the creek mud. One boy's pa owned a saloon, and the other was a good for nothing fellow. Mama did not want folks thinking I was like those girls, so she went out of her way to keep me away from liquor and the saloon.

11

On Friday nights, the Criterion would fill up with men from the mines in their ragged dusty clothes, and it would get "pretty raucous." Even though I was never allowed in the saloon on a Friday night, I would often sneak down the back staircase to peek at the customers.

Unlike other Joplin saloons, the Criterion didn't have gambling or women, just a lot of whiskey and its share of sordid characters. Most of Papa's customers were townspeople, but others were transients and miners who were just passing through Joplin.

It was a rough time to be making a living on the plains. Folks wanted to find their way in this world, and they needed money to eat, drink, gamble and enjoy the finer things. As to be expected, the drink brought out the worst in some people. Most people carried guns, and those who did weren't afraid to use them at the slightest provocation, especially when liquor was involved. Brawls and gunfights mainly happened at the saloons up the street that had gambling and, of course, easy women.

Papa maintained that the drink gave men something to do, a way that they could be "social" with one another. Still it was difficult to keep the Criterion stocked with liquor. Papa would usually order liquor from salesmen, and they would ship it from Chicago by railroad. Half the time the liquor was stolen during shipment. When he had a hard time getting his supply, Papa made his own or bought hooch from the fellas in town who had special recipes that brought in customers with a taste for homemade whiskey.

The temperance crusaders' goal was to outlaw liquor, plain and simple. They were all around Missouri at the time and very well organized. They believed that liquor turned a man into the devil himself. Papa said more than once that the crusaders were a royal pain in his ass, and he knew that they could put him out of business. But temperance was coming, he'd say, "like a freight train on the downside of a hill with no brakes."

When I was young, I wasn't allowed in the saloon at all, except sometimes on an early Saturday morning when no one was around, Papa would let me spend time with him in the saloon. We would go to the post office first, and the Newman General Store before heading back to the Criterion, which would be all closed up and quiet. Mama and Papa would do their chores while I twirled around on a stool behind the bar daydreaming about being a piano player someday in Papa's saloon. Gracie, my Scottish bull terrier, would lie quietly at my feet as I dreamed about wearing pretty dresses made of satin and lace, with my hair pinned up under a wide brimmed hat. In my dream, I would be singing my heart out as I played my piano for the folks in the saloon.

The saloon had no chairs, other than that stool behind the bar where I would sit. Papa said standing up kept the drunken men from getting into fights and smashing the furniture to "smithereens." Menfolk didn't care if they had to stand up when they drank whiskey and chewed tobacco.

The Criterion's long bar was made from beautifully carved walnut and had ten brass spittoons lined up in front on the floor. A big sign behind the bar read, *"All Nations Welcome But Carrie."* That sign had a special meaning to the saloon folks, but I had to grow up before I learned what it meant.

In 1901, Papa was in a saloon in Kansas City when Carrie Nation herself came in and took a hatchet to all the bottles of liquor in the bar. She was part of the temperance movement that was out to bring every saloon down. Carrie had her followers, who would sing righteous, God-fearing hymns while she swung her hatchet at every bottle in sight. Carrie Nation was so popular with folks that she started appearing in Vaudeville shows in which she loudly denounced the evils of liquor. She wrote her own newsletter filled with stories about the devilish things that liquor did to the good men of America. I am not sure what Papa would have done if Carrie and her followers ever showed up at the Criterion. It was bad enough for him to see her antiliquor newsletters being passed around in our town. Of course, everyone was forbidden to mention Carrie Nation's name in Papa's company.

People loved Papa for his storytelling, which usually centered on the Wild West. He told a story about Jesse James and Jesse's brother, Frank, coming into the Criterion one time. The James brothers had etched their initials in the top of the bar with a pocket knife, along with the words "Frank and Jesse were here, 1880." Of course, this happened before I was born and before Papa worked the saloon, but those initials and words were still in the top of that bar for all to see and touch.

4

Nothing that is worth knowing can be taught.
~OSCAR WILDE (1854–1900)

Papa earned a good living for us working the saloon. We had a nice home above the saloon, a barn, three horses, a large buggy, and a smaller one that I used. I was always dressed in the finest clothes that you could find in southwest Missouri because Mama and Aunt Maggie made most of my clothes. Mrs. Elizabeth Wildebrand was our housemaid. We called her Lizzie. She used to bring her daughter, Cora Jean, who was a bit older than me, with her when she came to help Mama.

I never met Cora Jean's father, but she sure told stories about him being a miner and striking it rich. She was convinced that he would come for her someday. I suspect she probably never met him or even knew who he was for that matter, but she could talk about him as if she did. Cora Jean did not have much in the way of things, but she was probably the kindest and most agreeable friend you could ever have. Cora Jean and I, and sometimes even Olive, would dress up with the old clothes that Mama set aside for the rummage. Sometimes we played school. Olive always played the school marm because she thoroughly enjoyed handing out difficult assignments to Cora Jean and me, her pretend students.

Cora Jean appreciated everything anyone did for her, so I loved to give her my dolls, and pretty clothes just to see her reaction. We had a lot in common, or so I thought. Cora Jean loved for me to read to her while she acted out the stories, and she would always dance and sing to my piano music.

For most children my age, piano lessons were just another chore, but not so for me. I was determined to be the best piano player that I could be so I could earn my keep playing the piano someday. There was little opportunity in southwest Missouri for a girl to make an honest living. You could make clothes, serve food, or work as a maid for the rich folk in the Webb City mansions as many poor folks did. And of course, there were the saloon ladies that I was not allowed to speak about. It wasn't a job I'd choose anyway because I heard that men paid those ladies for their attention. There wasn't much for me to do out here on the plains until music became my salvation and the piano, my path to it.

When I was fourteen, Mrs. Charlotte Crockett, asked me to play the piano regularly for the Grace Episcopal Church choir on Sunday mornings. I was a proud member of that choir and so were the other singers. They took their music seriously and could really sing out the hymns.

"Adella Marie Lawton, you are just the person I want to talk to," Mrs. Crockett said as she grabbed my arm in the hallway of the church one Sunday.

Facing me, she placed both of her hands on my elbows and leaned in a bit closer to my face. "You know…Mrs. Helms, the choir pianist, is retiring and moving back east."

"Yes, ma'am," I said.

"Now just who do we know that might do as Mrs. Helms's replacement, hmmm?"

Before I could answer, she continued, "I've been thinking. You really have become a very good player and…you play your hymns so well. What would you think about replacing Mrs. Helms?"

This was an exciting, but odd request. I was a saloonkeeper's daughter, and most church folk were dead set against saloons. Lucky for me, our church was not full of saber-rattling temperance women whose only goal in life was to keep their husbands out of saloons and off the drink. The women in my church tolerated Papa as a saloonkeeper better than most. With his strict rules about no women and gambling, they thought the Criterion was the lesser of three evils.

Serving as the choir's piano accompanist was what I had been praying for, but I sure didn't expect it to happen right then.

"I don't know what to say, Mrs. Crockett," stumbled out of my mouth.

"Well, I know I would have to talk to your folks and get their permission. I already mentioned something to your mama, and she suggested that I talk to you first."

I wanted to shout with joy, but I knew I should handle this situation maturely, as Mama and Aunt Maggie would expect. They always taught me to hold my tongue and not to speak my mind. People really did not want to know what a person really thought about things, good or bad. No, most folks were content to stay on the surface with people, they'd say.

"I would be honored to play piano for the church choir. You know that, Mrs. Crockett," I finally said in the most mature voice that I could muster.

Our church had a beautiful grand piano, and this opportunity would give me almost unlimited access to it. Of course, this also meant that I had to practice with the choir every Thursday night and go to church every Sunday, which would keep Mama happy. On Mondays, Mrs. Crockett would send Olive to school with a list of all the hymns for the following week's service, and I would spend the week learning and practicing them.

All those piano lessons had paid off. I was fourteen and had my first job with the church choir doing something I really loved. I didn't earn but a quarter a week, but I planned to save every quarter so I could buy new sheet music from Gottfried's mail order catalogue.

The Grace Episcopal Church had a great hall we called "God's Sanctuary" where all of the sermons were given. On Sunday mornings, we would sit in God's Sanctuary with all the other Episcopalians and learn what we had to do to avoid being condemned to hell for all eternity.

My mind always wandered during the service to the dark, majestic, mahogany piano that stood in front and to the left of the pulpit at the center stage. Father Pickett was short and bald, but he had a booming voice when he brought shame on all the sinners who came to his church while I daydreamed about the music that I would play at the end of his service.

The sanctuary windows had been beautifully pieced together with stained glass depicting scenes of Jesus and his disciples and glorious angels from heaven. By late afternoon, the sun would shine through the glass, and the light would color the great hall casting brilliant jewels of color throughout the sanctuary as music from my fingers filled the room. I played everything I could get my hands on from assigned hymns to classical music. Sometimes, in a quiet moment when no one was around, I would just improvise.

I didn't know what heaven was like, but playing piano in God's Sanctuary as colors from the sun lit glass danced off the walls almost seemed like heaven to me.

5

*Don't tell fish stories where people know you; but particularly
don't tell them where they know the fish.*

~MARK TWAIN (1835-1910)

Papa and his friends loved to go fishing at the Joplin Creek branch of
Turkey Creek on Sunday when there wasn't a baseball game at Miner's
Park on Third Street. He'd say that every hour of fishing and watching
baseball added a day to his life, and I believed him. It was a real nice walk
through the woods down to the creek on a Sunday afternoon. Most of the
time, he would bring home a whole bucket of catfish or rainbow trout
for Mama to clean and fry up for supper. I went with him in the buggy
to the creek many Sunday afternoons where I'd sit reading and drawing
pictures. Mama would use this time getting Sunday supper ready. Uncle
Sam would usually go with Papa and me, and sometimes we would meet
up with Harry McGinnis, the town constable. He was a young man for a
constable, but he liked to swap stories with Papa. Some years later, after we
left Joplin, Harry McGinnis and a younger constable, Mr. Harryman, were
murdered in Joplin by outlaws named Bonnie and Clyde.

Joe Robinson liked to fish with Papa, too. He was still working at the
Criterion as its porter helping keep the bar stocked and clean, and he took

care of our buggy horses, too. Joe helped Papa keep the saloon stocked, but he was not allowed to throw the drunks out on the street, when they got too disorderly, which was often when the miners were in town. Papa did that himself cause Joe was colored and no white man would let Joe touch him in these parts.

Papa enjoyed fishing with Joe because he seemed to intuitively know when and where the fish were biting. But the townspeople, and even the law, frowned on the whites mixing with colored people. The coloreds frowned upon their kind mixing with the whites. Everything in town, the churches, schools, restaurants, and saloons were set up to keep colored folk separate from the white folk. Our Supreme Court said that colored folk were to be separate but equal. The "Jim Crow" laws that applied to folks with any negro blood, kept the races separate, but they were hardly treated equal. Joplin built the Lincoln School in 1908 just for the colored children because they were not allowed in my school, but it was a known fact that the Lincoln School was far inferior to my school. Those Jim Crow laws didn't stop my Papa from being Joes' friend and Joe would do anything to help out my Papa.

Papa and Harry would talk about business in my presence, but half the time I had no idea what they were talking about. Even if I did, I would pretend not to listen. Reading my book was much more entertaining. Harry liked to talk about his stressful job, which he said was therapeutic. Being a bartender and all, Papa was always a good listener.

"You know, Mike…it's getting so bad that they're sayin' this town has become a pretty foul place to live," Harry told Papa on one occasion when Joe and I were within earshot. Uncle Sam had walked up the creek to fish his favorite hole. "I think the word is that our folk are 'terrorized.' These thugs aren't up to respecting the law. Somethin's gonna have to be done. Folks just don't feel safe here anymore."

"Who's callin' it that?" Papa asked out of the side of his mouth that didn't have his smoking pipe stuck in it.

"My sister sent me a newspaper article from St. Louis that talks about the lawlessness goin' on in Joplin. Makes it sound like we don't have any control here, with all the bank robberies, lynchings, murder, rapes, thefts, whorin'…"

Papa looked my way to see if I was listening, and I acted like I wasn't.

"That's certainly how it used to be here, but I didn't think it was so bad anymore… Sounds like you got your hands full," Papa said.

"Didya hear about Dan Ames?"

"Nope."

"He was bringin' in a load of wood to town last week, real early in the morning in his wagon. When he got to the end of the road, his horse spooked. It turns out there was a colored man hanging from the tree near the side of the road. If it weren't for the horse spookin', he'd never have noticed."

"Do you know who the colored was?" Papa asked. I glanced at Joe. I could tell he was listening by the look on his face, but Joe didn't say much when the constable was around. Then Joe stood up as slowly and nonchalantly as he could and made his way upstream to fish with Uncle Sam.

"Naw, we just cut that poor bastard down and buried him in a pine box in the cemetery," the constable said. "Somewhere somebody is probably looking for him."

"Well, people sure have their ways," Papa said shaking his head.

"You remember Thomas Gilyard?"

Papa looked at him dumbstruck.

"You know that fellow they lynched uptown," the constable explained.

I gasped and put my book down. "I remember that."

Papa looked over at me and shook his head.

"How do you know about that, young lady?" the constable asked.

"Well…I was there," I said with some pride, and with that, the secret was finally out.

"You are too young to have been there, Miss Adella," Harry said. "Now Mike, you didn't take this child over to watch that lynching like most of the folks in town, did you?" Harry said, rubbing his forehead with his dirty hand.

"Nope."

I looked over at Papa, and his eyes met mine. He knew.

"I was with kids walking home from school."

"Oh… I see," Papa said in such a way that I couldn't tell if I was in trouble or not.

"Why'd they lynch that man, Mr. McGinnis?" I inquired.

"Gilyard was no angel, Miss Adella. He was accused of killing Theo Leslie, a Joplin police officer, who had gone down to the rail yards to arrest a gang of thieves. Gilyard shot Leslie. People saw him do it. He was arrested and put in the jail downtown, but folks were not going to let that be. A mob broke through the jail walls and dragged him to the center of town where they lynched him. There were a lot of folks and their kids that came out to watch this lynching, which you already know if you was there."

"I think I saw Thomas Gilyard at the corner of Second and Wall that day. I remember seeing a rope," I said as the memory of that moment flooded my brain.

"That's really too bad, Miss Adella. You weren't s'posed to be see-in that... It's not the way the law s'posed to be. You hear?"

"What happened after they lynched him?

"That same mob kept tormenting the colored folk through the night by setting fires to their homes. When the firemen got to the fires, they found that their fire hoses had been slashed. Most colored folk in Joplin just packed up their belongings and left town."

"Not Joe, he was left behind," I said remembering the stories that I had heard.

"Joe stayed with us," Papa said.

"Lynching people before they go to the courthouse seems real wrong to me, Mr. McGinnis. Does this happen that way often?"

"Not too much...there was all that trouble a couple years ago over in Springfield. They lynched three colored men that day right in the town square. They say five thousand people showed up to watch that one."

Papa grimaced. "I heard bout that...What'd those boys do?"

"Some say they were innocent, but they were accused of assaulting a white woman. It took the governor of Missouri to send troops to Springfield to stop the violence. At least, we got a conviction in Joplin. Mitchell got ten years in the pen for lynching Gilyard. In most places, you can't get a jury to convict a white man for lynching a colored. It just won't happen 'cause folks don't care about the no-lynching laws in these parts."

"Do they only lynch colored people?" I wanted to know.

"Naw, lynching is color-blind, Miss Adella. I read somewhere that a white minister was lynched for being unfaithful to his wife. Other white folks been lynched too, even women."

"Papa, Mr. McGinnis, please...please don't ever let anyone lynch our Joe."

"No need to worry about Joe, Miss Adella," the constable reassured me, but when I looked over at Papa, he just looked away. Then they just sat quietly fishing for several minutes.

"You still havin' trouble with those Marcus boys, Mike?" the constable asked, finally breaking the uncomfortable silence.

"No more than usual," Papa mumbled under his breath. "Hey, anything biting over there, Harry?" I knew Papa was trying to change the subject.

I didn't know who the Marcus boys were, but I couldn't help but wonder what kind of trouble they were giving my Papa. A while later, I glanced over and saw a group of people in the distance gathered by the creek. There were men and women in a circle all dressed up, and each of them had a book in hand. They were talking to one another mostly, but every once in a while one of them would break out of the circle and run or play fight in the field.

"Who are those people?" I asked Papa, because I had never noticed people like this down at the creek, or in town.

"It looks to me like that's the theater folk," he replied.

"The theater folk?" I questioned.

"Yeah," the constable said, "they're the ones doing the show in town... some kinda play, I think. Heard it was pretty good."

"Oh, have you seen the play?"

"No, ma'am."

"Can we go over there and meet them?" I asked.

"I don't think so," Papa said.

"Why?" I questioned. "It might be fun."

"No, I don't want you around them kind a people. You're too young to understand. "

"What's wrong with them?" I said. Uncle Sam and Joe, who had returned from upstream, kept quiet this whole time.

"They're just different. They have different ways. That's enough questions," Papa curtly replied, and that was that.

I couldn't help but wonder what made the theater folk so different and wrong for me to meet. They were laughing and playing, and they looked like real happy people to me.

6

*Our professional connections insure the presentation of high class
and clean entertainment always, and our patrons may
rely on finding here a standard precluding any suggestion of
vulgarity or coarseness, and Mothers can send their children
with the utmost confidence.*

~THE MANAGEMENT

Joplin had a huge theater called the Club, which reminded me of a palace. It was built in 1891 by the Joplin Club, a group of rich townsfolk who wanted to bring culture to Joplin by building the theater and the Keystone Hotel. The Club Theater's auditorium was three stories high, with balcony seating, a large stage, an orchestra pit, and box seating for the rich folk. It was very luxurious in its time and seated 1400 people, big by Joplin's standards. The stage curtain had a colorful hand-painted picture of the Grand Falls at Shoal Creek. The Club not only offered entertainment, but patrons could get anything from whiskey to peanuts while they watched a show or attended a political event. There were two grand rooms for hosting special events on the second floor. The Club, which was at 402 Joplin Street, was just a few blocks from the Criterion.

On the Club's opening night in 1891, a half-crazed miner burst into the theater to find a girl who had just jilted him. When he did, he took a shot at her with his gun as she sat in her seat. Papa and Mama were there that night, and luckily, nobody got hurt, not even the girl who jilted the miner.

The Club soon became the center of Joplin's society, with music, drama, and political events for people to attend. In 1908, when I was eleven years old, William Howard Taft came and spoke at the Club during his election campaign. Mama took me to see President Taft speak; of course, it was before he was elected. That same year the Shubert Theatre was built right down the street from the Club. The Shubert brought in even more elaborate and expensive shows, but Mama and Aunt Maggie usually took me to the Club because it was more reasonably priced. By the time we were fourteen, Olive and I would try to make every show at the Club or the Shubert, if our parents approved of the show.

The Vaudeville shows that came to the Club featured a variety of acts, with jugglers, singers, and musicians. We saw one show with everything from a violin solo to artistic roller skaters and a musical barrel jumper. My favorite act was the "Buckley's Comedy Animals" where they would dress different animals in outfits and parade them across the stage. The "Roller Skating Bear" and "Delighted Teddy" were a few of the great Vaudeville animal acts that I remember. One show had an amazing juggler, who was also a comedian, too. One night Papa almost split wide open laughing at his act. Later Papa would say that this act had made him almost "split a gut." That funny man sure brought laughter to Joplin. He knew how to entertain the crowd so well that I believe he went on to become a movie star after Vaudeville.

The Vaudeville musicians could do amazing things with their instruments to bring joy to the crowds that flocked to see them. "Karl" was known as the "Wizard of the One String" because his instrument was made of only a cigar box, a pine stick, and one string. He could play so many different songs on that makeshift instrument that it was really something to see.

The piano players brought all of the popular music to Joplin, and the Club had another one of those beautiful upright grand pianos, which stood on the floor below the center stage. I remember the first time I saw that piano, with its jet-black cabinet and perfect ivory and black keys. Its sound was almost too beautiful to believe. Every time I saw it, I imagined what it would be like to walk up to it, sit down on the bench, and play. It was just a dream.

Vaudeville helped bring me to that dream as I watched the musical performances and dreamed of playing the piano. I loved the music, but Olive liked to go to the Vaudeville shows to flirt with the boys from school.

7

All the worlds a stage
And all the men and women merely players;
They have their exits and their entrances and
One man in his time plays many parts.

~WILLIAM SHAKESPEARE (1564–1616)

One Sunday in 1911 in the late afternoon shortly after my fourteenth birthday, Papa was fishing at the Joplin Creek. I stayed home with Mama while Uncle Sam and Maggie were at a church function. There was a knock at the door, and as Mama opened the door, Constable McGinnis appeared in the doorway.

"Where's Mike?" he asked, wasting no time with pleasantries.

"Now you know where Mike is, Harry...where he is every Sunday, at the creek, fishing."

"It seems we have a report of a possible break-in downstairs at the saloon, and I want him to go in there with me to check it out."

"Oh, hell," Mama said, so startled she could hardly get the words out of her mouth. She looked at me. "Della, you go on down to the creek and get your papa. Tell him that Harry came by with a report of a break-in and I went with Harry to the saloon. He needs to get back here right now."

I was still in my church dress, but changing into something else would have to wait. Joe went with me to hitch my horse to the small buggy.

"Miss Adella, you want me to take you to the creek to fetch your pa?" Joe asked me.

"No Joe, I'll go. You stay here with Mama."

When I approached the path to the creek, I tied my horse and buggy to a tree and ran as fast as I could down the crooked path to the water. Halfway there, I heard muffled voices, so I knew that someone was down at the creek with Papa.

When I cleared the path to the creek, I didn't see him, so I called out for him, "Papa!" Suddenly someone behind me tugged hard on my hair, and a hand clamped over my mouth as I struggled to turn around. Then another hand grabbed at my waist, and I could hear my dress rip. I could not see who was dragging me backward to the water's edge, but I saw another man I did not recognize holding a butcher's knife to Papa's throat. He was a seedy looking character with brown, greasy hair and a leathery, wrinkled face. His hooded eyes peered at me.

"Oh, so is this your young-in?" the man said snidely, eyeing me while pressing the flat side of the knife deeper against Papa's flesh. "I wonder how she would feel watching her daddy gettin' sliced. She a nigger-lover, too?" He spit in the dirt at my feet.

It was a good thing that Joe was not with me, I thought. These men would surely lynch him.

Papa said nothing. He just stared at me as his face grew beet red. I heard someone singing and glanced beyond Papa toward the field where the theater folks had gathered to practice, but today the field was empty. Then I noticed two more men in the distance stumbling toward us along the creek. Probably more of this lot, I thought. They were doin' the singing, as they stumbled and tripped over their feet. When one of them fell down, I knew they must be real drunk. Their hair was all messed up, hanging in their eyes, and their shirts were ripped open at the top. The taller one was carrying a stick, which did little to help him walk. The other one had a bottle of what looked like whiskey in his hand. They were barefoot with their pant legs rolled up as if they had been wading in the creek.

"Well, son of a bitch," said the man who was still holding me tight from behind. "Who are these clowns?'

"Forget 'em. They's just drunks. Pay 'em no mind," the one holding Papa captive said.

Then my attacker spun me around, throwing me backward against a nearby tree, its bark cutting sharply into my skin. I could still see the two drunks walking our way, but my attacker was facing me. I now could see what an ugly man he was, with his scarred face and dirty hair slicked back from his brow. He was sweaty and smelled like he hadn't bathed. His hand, wet from my tears and spit, still clamped on to my mouth—I would have bit him, I swear, if I could bear to put any part of his vile-tasting hand in my mouth. He also spit the brown chew juice down near my feet, making me feel sick.

"You gonna start cooperatin?" asked the man pressing the knife to Papa's throat as the two drunks drew nearer.

The tall drunk with the stick looked at me as if to tell me something with his eyes.

"Hey, you...you got anything to drink over there?" the other drunk slurred. Now it didn't seem like these fellows knew each other at all. "How 'bout some whiskey or moon...shine," he howled with laughter.

"You guys git outa here now. This ain't your bidness," said Papa's captor.

"Oh...excuse me, *sir*... We just wanna drink," slurred the shorter drunk losing his balance. The tall one reached out, managing to hold his companion up.

"Hey, mister...Do you know where we can get a damn drink?" the short man persisted as he approached the man with the knife, to my disbelief.

Then it all happened so fast. In one graceful move, the tall man swung his walking stick high landing it smack on the back of my captor's head, and I was instantly freed from his grip. He crumbled to the ground and was writhing in pain. The shorter man then seemed to fly through the air as he, drunk as he was, knocked the man with the knife right to the ground where the dirt met his face.

"Hey Vic...rope," the tall drunk said to his companion.

Gone was the clumsiness of a drunk that he seemed to be moments before. He now spoke in the most beautiful steady voice, with crisp articulated words and an accent that I had never heard before. He and his friend hogtied the men on the ground with the rope. Then he stood and looked at me, and I noticed he had the deepest brown eyes. He smiled as he reached out, and he ever so lightly touched my cheek with the back of his fingers. I just stood there in awe.

That was the first time I ever laid eyes on Clifford Hastings.

8

"We sent one of our ladies to get the constable," the tall man said to me. My new hero had suddenly become the most elegant man I had ever laid eyes on, and he was definitely not drunk. "He should be here any minute. These blokes looked like they really had it in for you," he said as he looked over at Papa.

Suddenly, it dawned on me that this man and his friend knew exactly what they were doing in pretending to be drunk. Their timing had been perfect, their movements precise. And in the end, would anyone have believed it was just an act and these seemingly wicked fellows were probably just actors who rescued us from a terrible fate.

The taller man and his friend positioned themselves over my assailants, holding them to the ground until the constable and his men showed up. Papa waited impatiently pacing back and forth. When Constable McGinnis arrived, Papa explained to him and his men all of the details of what had happened. One of the constable's men walked over to the man who had dragged me there, giving him a good kick in the gut and grounding his face in the dirt with his foot.

"You son of a bitch, you like to pick on little girls, do you?" was all he said to the bad man, who did not utter a word.

As the other law men began to close around those two, Mama came up and hustled me out of there. I never asked what happened to our captors, and Papa, well, he never brought it up.

For a long time after that, I had the most eerie feeling that someone was going to walk up behind me at any time and grab hold of my neck without me knowing it, and my heart would pound as I broke out into sheer panic. I didn't think I would ever grow back the nerve to walk down to Joplin Creek alone.

The following Tuesday I went back to school at Joplin High School. Labor Day, a relatively new holiday for the working man, had come and gone, and the new school year had begun. Olive hurried over to me when she saw me in the school hall.

"Della, I heard what happened to you. Are you okay?" she said, throwing her arms around me in a hug.

"No, I'm not okay. Would you be okay if a vile creature had his dirty, rotten hand in your mouth?"

Before I knew it, the other students were beginning to circle around to hear my story.

"Is it true that some fellas from the Club rescued you? Performers?" Olive asked.

"Yes, ah…I think so…it was something how it happened. They just showed up out of nowhere acting like they were drunk, and then, it was over and the attackers were on the ground being tied up. I think they were actors."

"Did you meet em?" Olive asked.

"Who? The men who attacked me?"

"The actors, silly."

"No, not really. Everything happened so fast." I kind of lied not wanting to share the special moment that I had with the taller man touching my cheek. I kept reliving that moment over and over in my head and trying to forget the rest.

"What do you mean, you 'did not really meet them'?"

"Well, we never were formally introduced. Then, the constable showed up with Mama and some others, and they were all busy talking. And Mama, seeing that my dress was torn, took me by the arm and hustled me away from there."

Olive stared at me wide-eyed in disbelief. She noticed the cut on my lip.

"I scraped my back on a tree. My lip was bleeding, too, from having that man's hand in my mouth."

"Don't you think you ought to thank those guys?" Olive asked with a sly smile. She was building up to something. "After school, let's you and I go down to the Club and see if they're around. Then you can thank them personally."

"Oh, I don't know about that," I said, just wanting to forget the whole thing.

"Oh, come on. Quit being a sissy girl."

I knew Olive was not going to let up on me until I agreed to go with her.

So after school that day, we headed to the Club Theater, presumably so I could meet and thank the gallant actors who had rescued me and Papa. It was all Olive's idea.

The Club was on the opposite side of town from school, so we decided to ride the trolley. Joplin had two trolley cars on the main street, and even though the ride cost a whole penny, it was great fun.

When we arrived at the Club, the front door was unlocked, so we stepped inside finding a dark theater lobby. No one was about.

"Hello," I called out. The sound echoed off the walls of the empty hallway. I actually hoped at that point that no one was there and we could leave.

We heard the echo of footsteps as a plain-looking woman came around the corner and greeted us. Her spectacles were down on the tip of her nose, and she wore a blue skirt and a white blouse with a crisp, white apron over the top. We could hear her footsteps echo off the walls in the great hall as she walked toward us.

"May I help you girls?" she asked, pushing her spectacles back onto the bridge of her nose.

"We're looking for people from the show that was here this past week-end," Olive offered, trying to sound older than she looked.

"Well, I'm afraid that show troupe has left town already. They're Vaudeville and they don't stay in any one place too long," the woman said.

"Oh...Well, thank you anyway," I said, turning to leave the building.

"You're welcome. Make sure you come on down with your friends for our next show." With that, the woman turned to leave.

"Ah, ma'am?" Olive was not going to let it go that easy.

"Yes?"

"What was the name of the Vaudeville troupe that just left?"

"They were part of the Orpheum-Keith Circuit...a large Vaudeville troupe."

"Will they be back?" I inquired more confidently.

"Well, I am not sure about that. Sorry, I really have no information on the schedule for any of these troupes that come through here."

It was becoming apparent to me that I probably would never get the chance to thank those performers for helping to rescue Papa and me from those villains by the creek. "Come on, Olive. I need to get home."

Olive didn't hesitate. "Hey, ma'am? Do you happen to have an extra playbill lying around from that troupe?"

"Hmmm, I don't know. Let me look." With that she turned and walked back down the hall, leaving us standing there alone. Olive noticed some papers on a ledge by the box office, and she walked over to the ledge, grabbed a paper, and stuck it down the front of her blouse.

"Let's go," she whispered. "I've got what we want." We could hear the lady's heels loudly approaching us as we headed for the door.

"Sorry, girls, I can't find anything on that troupe."

"That's okay," I said politely. "Thank you for trying."

When we got outside, Olive ran ahead of me twirling and skipping like a five-year-old. When we got at least a block away, she pulled the paper she had taken from her blouse.

"Program for Private Vaudeville Entertainment," Olive read aloud, *"At The Club Theatre, Joplin, Missouri. Midnight, August 31, 1911."*

No wonder I didn't see this show. It didn't start until midnight.

"Hurry up. Read the acts to me, Olive," I commanded.

"One: Overture by the Joplin Orchestra. Two: Violin Solo by Alfred Weaver Winston."

She was reading slowly just trying to get my goat.

I said, "I don't think he was an Alfred." She went on.

"Three: Kinodrome—latest patented film subjects. Four: Illustrated Song and Spot Light Melodies. Five: Frank Parrish—Musical Barrel Jumper."

"Wow!" she said. "Was he the barrel jumper?"

I reached to grab the page from her hand.

"Okay, okay," she said as she pulled away. *"Six: The Alpha Quintette— Miss Marion Lewis, Eugene Merrill, Cliff Hastings, Fred C. Ford, and Harry F. Vickery."*

"That's it…it's Vic! Harry F. Vickery. It has to be the one who tackled the guy by my Papa. Vic."

"Who is the one that helped you?"

"I didn't hear his name, but it must be either Mr. Merrill, Hastings, or Ford."

"Merrill, Hastings, or Ford," Olive repeated trying to commit those names to memory.

On the last day of September 1911, Cora Jean didn't show up at school, nor did she show up the following week or the week after that. One night I heard Mama and Papa discussing something in hushed tones that involved Cora, but they completely hushed up when I walked in the kitchen. Lizzie had stopped cleaning for Mama around that time.

When I asked where Lizzie was, Papa said, "Lizzie's gone and moved her family out of town."

The next week Mama had a new maid. She was colored, and her name was Nellie.

9

Spring rolled around bringing with it the spring school dance, and all the boys were competing for dates to the dance. Will Parker and Jake Sands kept showing up and vying for Olive's attention. She had accepted two dates to the dance, but had yet to decide which boy she was going to go with. Albert Jones eventually got around to asking me to go, and I reluctantly agreed to be his date.

Eventually, Olive decided on Jake Sands as her date, and the four of us decided to go together. I didn't have a lot of experience with boys; neither did Olive. Our mothers both impressed upon us that kissing boys was bad because it would lead to other things. Mama insisted that if you let a boy "have his way with you," no other boy would ever want to have anything to do with you. She said that a boy who is looking for a good time from a girl will promise her anything, but he would only marry a virtuous girl.

We were not taught about sex in school, nor were we taught about the consequences of sex, one of which was having children. We knew next to nothing about birth control because there was a federal law that prohibited the sending of birth control information or birth control devices in the mail. Birth control devices were often sold under the pretext that they were instruments that prevented disease, and no one was allowed to speak of the real purpose for the device. None of these subjects were spoken about in polite company and rarely spoken about with one's parents.

There was a lot of innuendo about the topic, but to a naïve girl like me, innuendo did not help me understand much. All I knew was that a boy and a girl could make bad things happen to the girl's reputation, and I didn't think I wanted any part of that.

So being with a boy like Albert at a dance was awkward. I was somewhere between being afraid of him and petrified, especially when it came time to actually dance with him. I suspected that Albert could sense my bashfulness.

"I thought I was the only one who couldn't dance," Albert said on the night of the dance.

"Oh, I can dance," I assured him. "It's dancing with you that I'm not sure about."

"That bad?"

"No, as long as you take it slow…maybe then you won't step on my feet." I was so tiny compared to him that most people would probably think that I was a little girl dancing with a grown man.

"Do you want to go do something else?"

"Not really. This is fine for now."

As it turned out, Albert had a flask of home-brewed whiskey in his pocket, what he called hooch. So Albert and I ended up sitting outside, on the ground sipping on hooch and telling tales. Olive and Jake stayed inside dancing to every dance.

"You're a really good piano player, Adella. Where did you learn piano?"

"At my church, mostly," I said, trying to hide my pride at his compliment. "I really want to get a job playing the piano when I finish school."

"You do? Why do you want to have a job?"

"What do you mean?"

"Well, usually the man gets the job and the woman stays at home."

"Why does it have to be that way? What about someone like me? I want to work. I want to have my own money."

Albert frowned.

"Are you going to college?" he asked.

"Mama says I might go to finishing school. Are you?"

"I want to be a lawyer like my father."

"That would be a good choice for you, Albert."

"I may want to be a judge someday."

"Better yet. It suits you."

"Think so?"

"Indeed, I do. You're always arguing with somebody about something."

"Well, being a lawyer is real important to me," he said, ignoring my jab.

"So is my music, Albert."

"Yah, but music is for fun, right? Being a lawyer is real serious business." He threw a stone across the school drive.

Albert's narrow mindedness was annoying me, so I set out to challenge him.

"You want to be a lawyer? Well, what do you think of lynching, Albert?"

He took a big gulp of hooch. "Depends. If the person has committed a crime and is sentenced by the law to a lynching, then I'm all for it."

"What if it's a lynching by just a few angry folk?"

"Well, I guess that kind of lynching would be wrong. What do you know about lynching anyway?"

Now it was my turn to take a swig. It tasted awful to me. "I saw a lynching, Albert." I said wiping the hooch off my mouth with my forearm.

"No way...Stop fibbing."

"Well, I did, except I didn't see the man actually get lynched, and I didn't see him die. But I saw his face, and I could tell that he knew he was about to die."

"You telling me the truth? " He looked me right in the eyes.

"Yes, I am Albert. Do you think it's ever right to kill a person?"

"If it's done according to the law.... executing a criminal? Well, yes."

"What if I don't think it's ever right to lynch someone because it's downright cruel?" Now I was looking him right in the eye.

"Adella, I don't know what you saw or why you are so bothered about lynching. It rarely happens, but when it does, the bum probably deserved it. Now I heard 'bout what happened to you at the creek. If I'd been nearby and had my gun, I woulda popped those guys for doing that to you. You, of all people, did not deserve what happened."

"You're talking about defending yourself with a gun, not lynching," I pressed.

"I sure am. Do you understand that killin' while defending yourself or in defense of others is justifiable under the law?"

"Yes, but it just seems morally wrong to me to kill unless there's no other way."

"Well you're just wrong, Adella. For all kinds of reasons, it is right to kill bad people. Trust me on that."

I was growing weary of this conversation. "Music is serious business to me, Albert. Trust me on that."

He stared at his half full flask of hooch. "You want to talk about music? I have nothing against music. My wife can play all the music she wants, for me and me only. I just wouldn't want my wife working outside the home playin' music somewhere for somebody else."

"Why not?" I demanded.

"It's just not right. It's not proper. It's the man that works, not his wife. She takes care of the children and the house. My mother doesn't have a job. My wife will not have a job."

"What if your wife wants to work?"

"No way. I want her home taking care of my business."

I was getting nowhere.

He held my hand for a little while. Once in a while, one of us would tell the other a story about the kids at the dance. When the dance was over, Albert walked me home, and I did not allow him to kiss me good night. Truth be told, at that point, I had not been kissed by a boy.

10

*Dreams are like stars: if you follow them they will lead you
to your destiny.*

~UNKNOWN

I often went to church with Mama and Papa on Sunday, but one particular Sunday in the summer of 1913 sticks in my mind. I remember playing the piano before and during the service. I planned to stay and practice for an hour afterward because I had a few new songs I wanted to learn. I was getting to the point where I could play from sight with little practice.

At the end of the service, I continued to play while the folks were leaving God's Sanctuary. As the crowd cleared, I happened to glance near the back pews and froze. There he was: the tall man with the stick who rescued me. His back was to me, but I thought for sure that it was him. It had to be. He was with a beautiful woman and a child, a little girl. They must have been performing again in the Vaudeville show at the Club. The girl had long, braided, brown hair and couldn't have been more than seven years old, I figured. The woman and the girl had fancy hats on and the most fashionable peach colored crepe and lace dresses with matching shoes, purses, and gloves. I could hardly believe they were here in my church.

I quickly sat down on the piano bench because that was about as far as my legs would take me. I couldn't help but think of Olive and what she would do if she knew he was here. Unfortunately, or maybe fortunately, Olive was nowhere around. She was probably downstairs getting the Girls' Charity Workers started on our next fund-raising project for the poor.

After careful deliberation, I chose the most beautiful hymn that I knew for the procession of the congregation leaving the church, "Gracious Spirit, Lord Divine." I played that hymn as well as I knew how.

If he looked my way, I hadn't noticed. When I finished playing, he was gone, and I was alone.

I hurried to meet up with Olive and the rest of the girls. The Girls' Charity Workers were planning to collect food and clothing for the poor. We had so many poor people in Jasper County, most of them women and children left behind by miners who'd moved on. They lived across the rail-road tracks, a part of town that we were never allowed to go visit. Our plan was to go house to house on this side of the tracks and collect clothing, food, and other things that people were willing to donate, and then we had to figure out a way to safely deliver our charity to the poor.

When I found Olive, she was talking to Betsy and Martha. They were members of the Girls' Charity Workers, too.

"Guess what?" I asked Olive, within earshot of Betsy and Martha who were listening intently.

"What?" Olive perked up.

"I saw him."

"What do you mean, you saw him? First of all, who...is him?"

"You know, him."

"Albert?"

"No, not Albert," I said, grabbing my Sunday hat and walking to the door of the church garden. "Let's go outside. I want to talk to you. Alone."

The garden was full of beautiful spring flowers, their sweet fragrance filling the warm air. Even the lilac trees were in full bloom. It was a sunny day, without a cloud in sight.

"Okay... tell me." The suspense was killing her, and I loved to be dramatic.

I sat down on a nearby stone bench. "Okay. I saw Merrill, Hastings, or Ford."

"No, you didn't. Where?"

"In church this morning."

"Our church?"

"Yes, our church."

"Did you talk to him?"

"I never had the chance. I was playing the piano," I said, shaking my head.

"So how do you know it was him?"

"I saw him. At least, I think it was him."

"Did he see you?"

"What do you mean, did he see me? I was playing the piano. He had to see me, or at least, hear me."

"Well, if he'd seen you, he probably would have run out the door." She laughed. "You should have run after him."

"Olive, he was with a woman."

"So?"

"A beautiful woman with a peach dress and matching hat, gloves…the whole outfit."

"So?"

"There was a child, a matching little girl."

"Matching little girl?" she repeated slowly.

"Yes, everything matched perfectly."

"Well, I don't think that means anything."

"How can you say that?" I asked, encouraged.

"He's a theater person, an actor or a singer. He travels all over and does shows. Those kinds of people don't get hitched. It's not allowed. I'll bet you that he's not hitched to that, that peach lady."

"What do you mean, they don't allow them to get hitched?"

"I read all about it. Those theater people have strict rules. The leading men aren't allowed to be married. That way all the rich, lonely, married ladies will flock to their shows hoping to get a date with one of them."

"Oh, it's no matter anyway. All I wanted to do was thank him, not marry him."

I looked at Olive. She was obviously scheming. "You are not dragging me back down to the Club."

"Well, if you keep thinkin' that way, you'll never get to meet him." With that, she patted me on the back and walked back into the church. We really did need to figure out how to get our charity work to the poor folks who needed it and not chase around to find some married actor down at the Club.

11

We know what we are, but we know not what we may be.
~WILLIAM SHAKESPEARE (1564-1616)

Olive and I finished high school in 1914. The last year of school had passed so quickly, or so it seemed. I'd had a lot of fun, especially with Olive, while she had fun with her various boyfriends. I swear she had a different one each week.

One Sunday afternoon, Olive and I were sitting on a blanket by Joplin Creek while Papa was fishing. We were trying to write out graduation letters because we were planning to have a graduation reception at the church.

"Have you thought about what you're going do once we graduate?" she asked as she wrote out a letter.

"I've thought about it a lot," I said. "It seems that all I do is think about it. Nothing makes sense."

Not having a vision of my future was annoying me. Some people knew exactly what they were going to do, like Albert, for instance, while I felt like I was in a fog. The only thing I had figured out was that I probably would not be Mrs. Albert Jones, not unless he opened his mind. Whatever I did would have to involve music—I knew that much. In 1914, in Joplin,

Missouri, the opportunities for anyone, much less a girl, to be a paid musician were pretty scarce.

"Yeah, well I'm confused, too," Olive agreed. "And the more thinking I do, the more confused I get. My mom and dad want me to either get married or go to finishing school. Those are my choices: marriage or finishing school," she said curling up her nose.

"Both sound like a bore to me," I said. She nodded her head in agreement.

"What about you and your music, Della? Are you going to keep up with it?"

"I could never give that up. I think, or at least I used to think, that I might like to go on to college and be a music teacher."

"That would be a good career. Teaching might be fun, too."

"But for now, I'm not sure what I want to do. I hate all of this indecision. I really, really in my heart of hearts want to find a place to play my music. I not only want to teach, I want to entertain. I think I always have."

"Well, do it then."

"It's not that easy. Papa and Mama would have a fit if I just went out and joined a Vaudeville troupe."

"Whoa, slow down. Who said anything about joining Vaudeville? That life, oh my, I cannot see you doing all that traveling, show after show. It would not be suitable."

"I need to do something, and it has to involve my music. I want to play music, perform, entertain, wear pretty clothes, travel to exotic and wonderful places, meet creative, educated people, and enjoy my life. I don't want to be stuck here. But I know I'd never survive the life of Vaudeville," I sighed.

"I see you performing. I really do. I can't help but think that something good will happen. Opportunities will present themselves. You'll see. You just have to think about what you want and go get it. Don't let anything stand in your way. That's what my pa always says to the boys."

Olive was more optimistic about my music career than I was. She was probably the only person in this world that understood what music meant to me.

After graduation, Olive left Joplin to visit her aunt, May Beth Crockett, in Kansas City. She was going to be gone a month, a whole month, maybe longer. Will and Jake and many of the other boys from our class signed up for the army, and off they went to places that I probably would never have the chance to visit. They were all hoping to go fight in the war that had erupted in Europe. Every time a group of them would leave, they'd get a send off with a steak dinner at the House of Lords.

Olive and I were fixin' to go to finishing school in Kansas City in September, so we could learn how to be sophisticated ladies. My private plan was to find a music course where I could continue to learn and maybe become a music teacher. I did not expect to have the chance or the gumption to join a Vaudeville troupe and be a performer. I had nearly stopped thinking about the actors that rescued Papa and me at Joplin Creek.

After Olive left for Kansas City, I must have moped for a whole week. Mama and Aunt Maggie were becoming more and more concerned about me, so Mama tried to keep my mind occupied by giving me things to do. We made tiny cakes for the church bake sale that I helped decorate with yellow colored frosting made of sugar and butter. Aunt Maggie took me shopping, and we rode on the trolley. We picked out fabric so she could sew summer dresses, and we went to the library. Mama, Maggie, and I even went to a play at the Club Theater one Saturday night, where we saw Miss Irma Lehman and Mr. Clyde Hyer perform *A Daughter of the South*. It was billed as a "corking good play," and I have to admit, it was pretty good. At least I enjoyed it—I am not so sure about Mama. Aunt Maggie loved the theater and would enjoy just about anything it had to offer.

"Della, you can play a tune on the piano better than any of them," said Aunt Maggie, who always had words of encouragement for me. "You remember that, young lady, and don't let your Aunt Maggie down," she'd say and I would smile and give her a hug.

Probably, the most fun I had was getting dressed to go to the theater. It was Saturday night, and I felt like doing it up really good that night. So I put on a beautiful blue dress with creamy white lace and a sheer cover up that Aunt Maggie made for me. It was July, and I was almost seventeen. I even painted my face with rouge and lip and eye colors, and spritzed myself with rose petal perfume.

When I looked in the mirror, I thought I looked "like a million bucks," as Papa would say, but I didn't feel it. Something was missing and definitely wrong with my life, and no matter how good it was, I felt upside down. I had too many unanswered questions. I felt that my chances were limited, and if I wasn't careful, I was going to end up working the third floor down at one of the saloons as a night lady or "whore," as Olive called them. But even that was impossible because men scared the heck out of me.

This discontent kept me from sleeping that night, or maybe it was the dream that I could somehow be in the theater. I was a musician, a pianist, and all I needed was an audience. How can you truly be a musician without an audience? At night, my self-doubting seemed to find its way in. Was I good enough for a real audience? My mind gravitated toward those thoughts until I thought my head would burst. Then I would dream that I was running down Joplin's Main Street, trying to catch the trolley, but it was always ahead of me, and I could never quite get to it. I'd wake up and could not go back to sleep.

12

It is never too late to be what you might have been.
~*GEORGE ELIOT (1819-1880)*

Sunday morning did not come soon enough. I was up early that morning and dressed for church. Mama and I climbed into the buggy; Papa was already up in his seat waiting patiently.

"Della, you sure look tired," Papa said, glancing back at me.

"I am."

"Well, there were some folks from the Club Theater in the saloon last night. They were talking that the piano player there is leavin' his job for the summer. I think Jenkins is the manager's name. Somethin' like that... He comes into the bar once in a while. A real nice fella. Anyhow...they're fixin' to hire someone to take over the piano playin' job, but just for the summer. They asked 'bout you, Della. I told them you played for the church, but I had no idea whether you were interested in a summer job at the Club."

My eyes must have been as round as saucers. "You're teasin' me, right? You never said you had no idea if I would be interested, did you, Papa?"

"Well, I told them I would talk to you about it, and if you were interested, I would bring you down there first thing on Monday to talk to this fellow Jenkins. They have a troupe coming in next week to do plays, and

I think they're fixin' to hire someone right away. I figure it would pretty much take up most of your summer."

This was a turn for the better. "I'm interested," I said. "Yes, I am interested," I said without hesitation.

On Monday morning, I was up and dressed in the prettiest summer frock I owned, with a hat to match. Yes, it was important that I match. My shoes were white, and the dress was white with blue flowers. Aunt Maggie helped me fix my hair with the sides pinned up in braids under my hat. She thought it made me look older this way. Mama made the dress, and it was every bit as good as store bought.

"I guess I'm ready," I said nervously to Papa when I saw him.

"Do you have your music?" Papa asked out of the side of his mouth he had stuffed with a pipe.

"Yes, right here in my portfolio."

Papa loaded me into the buggy, and we headed down to the Club.

When we arrived, he helped me down from the buggy and told me to go on in, alone, pointing the way. Mr. Jenkins was in his office behind the counter when I walked in. A different lady was with him, who I thought must be his secretary.

"Hello, I am Adella Lawton," I told her, holding out my hand. "I'm here about the piano job. I believe I am supposed to see Mr. Jenkins."

"Oh yes, Adella. I'm Emily, Mr. Jenkins's secretary. I think he is expecting you. Just one moment."

Emily, who was quite a beautiful woman, slowly walked back into Mr. Jenkins's office. Tall and slender, she had a rather large bust that was not hidden under her tight shirt. She wore her hair braided and wrapped in a knot on her head, and she wore a lot of makeup that emphasized her big brown eyes. Her skirt came to the middle of her calf, exposing a good part of her leg, which was bare all the way down to her high-heeled shoes. I recognized her as someone that I had seen around town, but I was sure she didn't go to my church.

I felt fidgety standing there until Mr. Jenkins came out. A middle-aged man, he certainly was not princely looking, despite the fact that he was wearing a fashionable, navy pinstriped suit, a spotless white shirt, and navy vest, capped off with a dark red bow tie.

"Hello, Miss. Lawton. I was hoping that I would see you today. I spoke with your father on Saturday. Let me take you to the piano." He shuffled

out of the room expecting me to follow him. When we entered the auditorium, it was dark, quiet, and frankly, a bit unnerving, especially since I
really did not know these people, and they weren't exactly the church choir
type. I had no idea what to expect until I saw the upright grand piano in
the center on the floor in front of the stage under the gas lights where it
always had been.

"Please, Miss Lawton, have a seat at the piano. Take your time and
warm up. Then I want you to play me something. Anything you want,"
Jenkins said as he smiled. "By the way, Miss Lawton, you are eighteen,
right?"

I hesitated a moment. "Almost, sir, I know I look young for my age,
but that's because I am not quite five feet tall. I probably look like I'm still
in high school, but I'm not."

I was rambling, and he noticed my hands were trembling. "Just a few
jitters from my nerves, Mr. Jenkins," I explained. "I've never done anything
like this before."

"Okay, good," he said. "I will give you about ten minutes to get situ-
ated then."

"Thank you," I said, but he was already hurrying his way back to the
lobby. I needed all of that time to ready myself. But Mr. Jenkins was back
at my side in no time.

I wondered what kind of music he'd want to hear—something popular
or something classical? I chose something popular, "Telling Lies" by Irving
Berlin and Henrietta Belcher. Then I played, "Dear Mayme, I Love You" by
Irving Berlin. I finished with "All That I Ask of You Is Love," by Edgar Selden.
These were songs that had been popular a few years ago, and I knew them well.

"Very good, Miss Lawton. Very good," Mr. Jenkins said. "Now play
this," he said, handing me some sheet music I had never seen before. The
piece did not have a title, but it appeared to be classical music. I played one
page, and he nodded in approval. He was obviously testing whether I could
play on sight.

"So are you truly interested in coming to work for the Club Theater this
summer season, Miss Lawton? Depending on the performances, we often
have a pretty grueling schedule."

"Can you tell me about it?" Not that I really cared that the schedule
was grueling.

"Well, it varies by week, but Friday, I expect the Garside's Stock Company. They're going to start with a new comedy, *Ocean to Ocean,* and then I think they're going to do the play—it's a melodrama, *The Devil's Kitchen.* They will be here two weeks with two plays each week. I believe they are coming in from Paducah, Kentucky, on the noon train. I'll need you here Friday afternoon and evening for a while. Then I expect they will rehearse Saturday morning and try a run through of the first play Saturday afternoon. Depending on how far they get, probably more rehearsal on Saturday night then show time on Sunday night. You'll have Sunday day-time off, unless, of course, they need you for a rehearsal. They'll run the first play Sunday night, probably two matinees on Monday and Tuesday, of course Monday and Tuesday night. Then on Wednesday, it starts again with a new play. Probably the same schedule. It's hard for me to say exactly when or if they will need you. Depends somewhat on whether they have specialties between the acts. During some of the performances, the musical accompaniment is a small orchestra, but they will want you to play as well."

"Specialties?"

"Yes, well, specialties are small Vaudeville-type acts that some of the actors do between the acts of the play. Some sing, some dance—it's very entertaining, especially this troupe. They have been having a great run, and we are fortunate to have them, a very popular troupe in these parts."

"So for now, you need me here Friday afternoon. What time?" I asked.

"How about two o'clock? That'll give them time to get settled in here."

"Where do they stay?"

"Emily's got them booked in one of the local boarding houses that are within walking distance from here."

"I take it that they have the music?"

"Yes, but I will need you to fill in with some of your own music sometimes so make sure you bring plenty of songs with you." I sure had no problem with that.

"Thank you, Mr. Jenkins. I will see you Friday at two," I said, shaking his clammy hand. I had only a few days to get myself ready for this, but it was just what I wanted. Right?

Olive would kill me if I didn't... "Oh, Mr. Jenkins." I turned around. "Who is in the Garside's Stock Company?"

"Well, I'm not sure of all of them—they switch companies so frequently...But you have Harry Vickery and Cliff Hastings. Those two are always together. Oh, yes, Fred Ford and Eugene Merrill, wonderful actors. They do a superior job with anything they touch. I think Emma Warren is in the company. Marion Lewis, and yes, there's a Miss Eunice Vickery and a Miss Sauncey Merschon, a Mr. Frank Merschon...a Mr. Charles Henshaw and a Miss Elise Claredon. I believe she and Mr. Hastings do the specialties, as well. That's all I can think of, though I believe Garside himself takes on a part or two in his shows sometimes." He was rambling off other names of performers, but I really stopped listening to a word he was saying after I heard him mention Merrill, Hastings, and Ford.

My head was swimming, again. I needed air. "Okay, very good then... I will see you at two on Friday, Mr. Jenkins." I turned and walked to the theater door.

"Miss Lawton," he said.

"Yes." I turned. "You might need this." He handed me a key. "Please stop by and see Emily to fill out some forms, for taxes, and the pay will be, at least to start, twenty cents per hour, and you must keep track of your hours on a card and submit them to Emily every Thursday. You will be paid on Friday. Oh, and feel free to come here and practice any time you like as long as nothing else is going on."

"Okay. Very good." I turned again to leave. Where was Olive when I needed her?

13

Our doubts are traitors, and make us lose the good
we oft might win, by fearing to attempt.
~WILLIAM SHAKESPEARE (1564-1616)

"Merrill, Hastings, or Ford," Olive's words kept repeating over and over in my head. One of them saved my life. Now I am about to meet all three of them and work with them. Can I really do this? I was starting to get a case of creeping self-doubt. *"Pull yourself together, Della."* I could hear Olive saying that to me. *"You have the talent, Della,"* she would say. *"Make them reckon with you."* Then she would say, *"Anyway... always remember they are just people like you and me. They have to brush their teeth and go to the pot every day just like you and me."* God love Olive. She would remind me that *"The only difference between you and them is you're younger and going to live longer. Don't you dare think those people are better than you. Make them earn your respect. You have worked hard for your talent."* These were all Olive's words, and they were all swimming in my head.

Friday was a sticky hot, summer day. It must have been near a hundred degrees. I took a long bath and put on a cool summer dress, another white one. I tied the sides of my hair in a knot on top of my head and let the bottom hair hang loose in soft curls.

Papa took me to the Club on Friday. It seemed like an eternity until we got there. He helped me out of the buggy and told me to walk right home when I was done that night.

The theater lobby was quiet as I walked through it, but when I opened the door to the auditorium, I found myself in the midst of a bustle of activity. Men were carrying in trunks, costumes, scenery, furniture, and more trunks through the open back door, while others were just milling around.

"Miss Lawton, you are just in time to meet some of the players," Mr. Jenkins said, hurrying to my side. "Garside, this is our pianist. Miss Lawton, this is Mr. Garside."

"Hello there, young lady. Glad to have you aboard," Garside said as he turned to yell at a stage hand. "Hey, you...move that furniture out of the way. Be careful with those flats. Lift that drop! Put that wall over there!" Then Garside walked to the front of the stage to shout more orders to the people standing up there.

Someone took my hand to shake it.

"Hello, Miss Lawton. I'm Harry Vickery. Just call me Vic."

"How do you do, Vic? It is a pleasure to finally meet you. Please call me Adella." I immediately recognized Vic as the man who rescued Papa at the creek.

"Wow. You're a beauty. It's not often we get to work with such a pretty piano player, Miss Lawton. Most of 'em got a beard if you know what I mean," he chuckled. "The pleasure's all mine. Let me introduce you to the rest of the cast. You can meet them while they're still civil."

"Good idea," I said.

Neither Hastings nor Ford were in the theater, but I did meet Merrill, and I realized that he was not my rescuer. An actress by the name of Miss Marion Lewis was lovely, and I thought she might have been the one in church in the peach dress.

Garside walked back over to me, handing me a huge folder. "Lawton, here's a copy of the first play we are doing, along with the music you'll need to play. It is marked in there when you will need to play each piece by number. Take some time to look through this and learn the musical pieces. Be prepared to play within the hour," he said and then he was gone.

"Hey," shouted Vic, "you're going to make her work now?"

"Someone has to work around here," Garside sneered as he walked across the room.

I found my way to the piano bench, trying not to trip and drop all of the music in my hands. Luckily, when I sat down, I felt right at home. At least I felt like I was in a safe place. The only thing missing was a bench pillow. I slowly read through the music hoping there was nothing too difficult. The specialty acts were Mr. Hastings and Miss Claredon. The songs that they sang were new to me, but nothing too difficult. I could hardly imagine having to play a part in the play and then sing and dance between acts on top of it all. I had been to plays and Vaudeville shows, but I had never experienced the two performed together, without giving the performers a break. This must have been what Mr. Jenkins met by "grueling."

The performers formed a circle of chairs on the stage, where they sat, playbooks in hand. There were a few playbooks in a pile on the floor. Two men walked from the back of the stage to join the group. One was whistling a tune to a song I had never heard.

Vic slapped the whistler on the back so hard it almost knocked him off his feet.

"Bloody hell, ready to get this show on the road, old chap?" Vic said, mimicking an accent.

This man was stunningly handsome, and he projected such confidence as he walked onto that stage. He was wearing a white hat, with a pencil tucked over one ear. The sleeves of his white shirt were unbuttoned and rolled up to his elbows. He looked so slender in his black trousers, and he seemed taller than the other men in the group, at least a foot or so over me. Something about him seemed familiar.

"If this bloody show is ready for the road, my name is Woodrow Wilson," the man replied with a smirk.

I knew that voice and that accent.

14

He's one with just the sweetest smile,
And one we all adore;
You bet his smiles are the very thing
To win hearts by the score.

Oh! How I would like to meet him
And shake him by the hand,
And say, "Cliff Hastings, believe me,
I think you are simply grand."

~Miss I.H.A., City
Des Moines Iowa, August 25, 1913.

I quickly turned my gaze down to the sheet of music, trying hard to stay focused.

"Where the hell were you, Cliff?" Vic sneered.

"Needed to see the barber, old chap. It would do you good to try it sometime," he bantered back.

"Why do you need a barber? You never take off your hat, and you certainly ain't manly enough for a shave."

Cliff sneered at him and grabbed a playbook off the floor before sitting down.

"How are you today, Cliff?" one of the ladies asked, gushing over him.

"Glad to be on this side of the dirt," he quipped. Everyone laughed.

"Okay. Heads up," Garside interrupted the banter. "Let's get this show on the road. Vic, quit picking on the talent."

Cliff nodded at Garside. Then he glanced down at me, and our eyes met for the briefest second. He smiled and nodded at me and then sat back down.

He was dashing and had the most wonderful smile. This was going to be the longest day of my life.

The play was *Ocean to Ocean*, a dark comedy. Garside started the rehearsal by explaining the play as a "sensational melodrama." Once the rehearsal got underway, the actors just read their parts. It was all business. Everyone had a part, and all the characters were of different nationalities and had different accents. No one broke character even at the first run-through. Every once in a while, Garside would interrupt to give someone instruction, but not very often.

Ford and Vickery played many small, odd character parts. Miss Lewis played a street waif, "Bowery Mamie," a rough character for such a gorgeous actress. Cliff played an energetic sailor who had just returned from the Philippines, which suited him. Miss Sauncey Merschon played "Crazy Kate," and Frank Merschon played a mean Mexican who hunted women. Even Garside got in the act playing a Chinese man or "chink" as he was referred to in the script.

The play had three acts. I had to play the piano between each act, for the "specialties," and during each scene change.

After the first read-through of the script, the stage blocking began. The actors took a short break at six o'clock, and a light dinner was brought in. One of the stage hands brought a cup of beef stew, along with a piece of bread and a cup of hot tea to me at the piano. We kept working until about eight o'clock when Jenkins reappeared. He spoke briefly with Garside, who was nodding his head, before walking over to me at the piano.

"You can call it a day for now, Miss Lawton. You have done a great job for your first day. Please be here at nine sharp tomorrow morning to practice the specialties." Jenkins turned and walked briskly back out of the auditorium.

As I was packing up my things to leave, I heard someone whistle. It was Cliff, who had whistled to one of the stagehands. They spoke for a second, and before I knew it the stagehand was at my side. All I could think of was that I had done something wrong.

"Is someone picking you up here at the theater, Miss Lawton?" he inquired.

"No, I'm going to walk home."

"Well," he said, "I've been instructed to accompany you safely to wherever it is you are going. My name is Pete." He extended his hand to me.

"Thank you. But that really is not necessary, Pete."

"Well, but if you don't mind, all the same, those are my orders."

"Your orders?" I looked for Cliff and found him busy working with Vic and Marion Lewis on a scene. "Okay. It's really not that far," I said.

"Then it will be no bother to me," he said as he followed me out of the theater. I felt like I was being watched as we left the auditorium.

I showed up for the specialties rehearsal on Saturday morning at nine o'clock sharp. The performers, Miss Elise Claredon and Cliff, were sitting side by side on the piano bench plucking away at the piano. She was dressed in a light cotton skirt and shirt, much like I was, and her blonde hair was fixed in a braided knot. Cliff was dressed casually as well in dark trousers and a white shirt with a bowtie. His sleeves were again rolled up to his elbow, and a pencil was tucked behind his ear. They made a handsome couple sitting on my piano bench.

"Looks like someone really wants my job," I said walking up to the stage.

"Miss Lawton, lovely to see you today! We actually don't want your job," he said with a smirk. "We just don't want to muff this up and have you booing us off the stage."

"Not like that is a real probability, Mr. Hastings. You don't get to be the popular leading man that you are by being a hick." I was trying to compliment him.

Elise chimed in, "I'm not sure that he was referring to himself being booed off the stage."

"What? You really think I'm an egotistical old bloke?"

"I know you're an egotistical old bloke, Cliff. That's why you have to have everything perfect," she said. Cliff laughed.

"Of course, you realize that doesn't take much effort on my part," he said, rising from the bench.

"Cliff, if you weren't so charming, I'd punch you right in the nose," Elise said.

"And if you weren't so annoying, I'd probably let you. Now look," he said, "it's already ten past and we haven't even sung a note. Please do get up off the bench Miss Claredon and permit Miss Lawton to take her rightful place at her piano."

With that, she rose from the bench, thrusting her sheet music at me before making her way to center stage.

"So do you think you can play this music? Have you ever played it before?" Elise asked as she frowned at me.

Miss Claredon was challenging me to a duel. She handed me the music to "How Can You Love Such a Man," by Irving Berlin.

"No, I have never played this song before, and yes, I can play it for you." Cliff arched his brow and smiled at me, approvingly.

"That's great, a piano player who doesn't know my song," Elise huffed.

"Even though she's never laid eyes on your song, Elise, I bet she knows it better than you," Cliff offered in my defense. He was definitely championing me in this duel.

He put a hand on my shoulder and whispered, "Don't worry about her. She can be a witch, but once you get to know her, you will find a heart of gold." His hand lingered on my shoulder a few moments longer.

I played the song for her perfectly the first time through. Her voice was very sultry, and I thought she would be fun to watch if I could take my eyes off the music.

"Well done," Cliff said when she had finished.

"Thank you," Elise said nodding to him.

"I was talking to Miss Lawton." She glared at him and sat down in the front row of the auditorium.

Cliff first sang "Dear Mayme, I Love You," another Irving Berlin song. His rich voice filled the room as he sang it with such emotion.

Then they danced and sang a duet to another Irving Berlin tune, "Herman Let's Dance that Beautiful Waltz." They moved together with

such perfection, you would have thought they had been singing and dancing together forever.

"Have you been doing this act together for long?" I asked.

"Oh, it's just a part of our Vaudeville act," Elise said nonchalantly.

Cliff was busy reading something and ignored us.

By ten o'clock, the other cast members began coming in from different
directions. Meanwhile the stage was being transformed into a scene with
furniture and lights.

"That's a wrap. Thank you, Miss Lawton, for your wonderful accompaniment," Cliff said.

Elise walked up on the stage, taking his arm and tugging it toward her.
They disappeared beyond the stage proscenium.

My first truly professional piano accompaniment was over, and I
thought I had done a pretty damn good job. I enjoyed it so much, in fact,
that I could have spent the whole day rehearsing with them.

The company kept me around for the better part of the day. In the
afternoon, a small orchestra joined us, and we spent a good deal of time
figuring out which parts each of us would play. There would be an evening
dress rehearsal at seven, after which Mr. Garside said they would probably
run through it two more times.

I thought the first dress rehearsal went well, but you'd never know it
listening to Garside. He had criticism for everyone, and of course, he delivered it like a tactless monster. It's a good thing he said nothing to me. I
probably would have burst out crying.

15

The only thing worse than being talked about is
not being talked about.

~Oscar Wilde (1854-1900)

On Sunday, I was to be at the theater at five to warm up. The show started at seven. I had been tired the night before and slept well, but Sunday morning came sooner than I had expected. Papa, Mama, and I went to church with Aunt Maggie and Uncle Sam. I played a few hymns during the service. Cliff was not in church, but I couldn't help but look for him. After the service, Mrs. Crockett told me the good news that Olive was due back from Kansas City on Tuesday.

I spent the rest of the day getting ready for the big night. I dressed in a black floor length skirt that Mama had made with my favorite white lace blouse. Aunt Maggie carefully pulled the sides of my hair up in a black ribbon, letting the rest of it cascade in curls made from the rags she had tied in my hair the night before.

By six thirty, the theater was packed with a lot of people that I knew; many seemed surprised to see me at a piano that wasn't in our church. I felt proud and honored to be there. Yes, I thought, this would be a good night.

The play went on without a hitch. The audience loved the show, especially Marion and Cliff's performances. Whenever he appeared on stage, the audience cheered and applauded. There were four curtain calls, and Garside allowed me to take a bow with the orchestra.

I saw Vic wandering around the stage looking for something after the show.

"It was a wonderful show," I said to him, packing up my music.

"Yeah, well let's see what the critics think in the morning paper. Hopefully, it will be a good review, and we'll pack 'em in again tomorrow." He quickly walked off.

So that's what success was all about in the theater. A play wasn't good unless the critics said it was good? What if the critic was a hack? Most newsman that I'd ever met, at least in these parts, were underhanded or slick Willies. They were always looking for the story to sell the papers no matter how newsworthy it was or wasn't. You could probably pay some of these guys for a good review. I don't doubt that some of that went on.

"I think you are really making a bloody mistake, Garside," I heard Cliff say angrily. He was standing near the back of the stage where it was so dark that I hadn't noticed his presence.

"Listen, Cliff, I'm going to try this. We'll show the movie clips between acts. If it doesn't work, then we'll do something else. We can always put the specialties back in. It's all about money, and they tell me this will help bring it in," Garside explained, nonchalantly.

"You know," Cliff said, "movies will be the bloody end of us." He briskly walked away leaving Garside standing there with his back to me.

I sure as hell did not want him to turn around and see me eavesdropping. I quietly, but quickly left the theater through a side door leading to a dark alley.

"What makes you think you can sneak out the back door?" I jumped. Cliff was standing just outside the door, leaning against the wall and smoking a cigarette.

"You startled the heck right out of me," I said, dropping some of my music on the ground.

"You startled me, too. I was hoping it wasn't one of my adoring fans." He smiled and with his cigarette in his mouth he bent down to pick up my music sheets.

"Nope, just me," I said as the butterflies took over my stomach.

"So are you saying you're not one of my adoring fans? Why aren't you going through the front door so you can enjoy some of the limelight, too?"

"Hey, I'm not in the company. This is your limelight."

"Want a smoke?"

"No, thank you. You know, Mr. Hastings…"

"Cliff," he said.

"Cliff…You really were great tonight. They love you out there."

"I sure wish I could see myself through your eyes."

"That would be an interesting experience, for both of us." I nodded. Our eyes met, and we stared at each other for a long moment. I wanted to ask him about the words he had with Garside.

"Is everything okay?" I hedged.

Before I could get a response, the theater door opened and Marion peeked her head out.

"There you are, you rascal. Garside wants everyone out in the lobby to sign autographs. Are you hiding from your fans again?" she asked Cliff.

"No, I'm hiding from you," he said, stubbing his cigarette out on the ground with his foot.

"Come on," she said, taking his arm and trying to pull him through the door. He wiggled out of her grip, stepped aside, and looked right at me.

"Ladies first," he said with a slight bow my way.

"Oh no, you go ahead. I've got to get going. See you both tomorrow." He smiled at me and nodded.

"Good night then, Miss Lawton," Marion said as she pulled Cliff with her through the door.

I walked around to the front of the theater, where I could see inside the window to the lobby where a crowd of people, mostly women and girls, had gathered. Cliff and Marion entered the lobby, with her now on his arm. The fans surrounded them, and playbills and pens were thrust toward Cliff's hand. He certainly was a popular leading man, and he played to his fans well, too.

The review that appeared in the newspaper turned out to be pretty good as reviews go.

GARSIDES THRILL BY REAL MELODRAMA

Pistols flashed and stilettos glistened with alarming frequency at the Club Sunday night, and the quietude of the Sabbath evening was punctuated intervalically with moans of love-laden ladies torn ruthlessly from the arms of their swains by inconsiderate and wholly informal Chinese gentlemen, residents of the chop suey and joss-stick sections of New York and San Francisco.

Lots of Excitement

"Ocean to Ocean" was the name of the agitation, and from the comprehensive expanse of the title, one was justified in expecting many startling vicissitudes, not the least of which came when the hero, after refusing to let his fiancée be sacrificed for him, was surreptitiously lowered into the snake pit, which the villain proceeded to describe with the effect of sending creep sand chills scurrying unceremoniously up and down the vertebrae of the more timid ones in attendance.

Marion Lewis was as tough as they make 'em as Bowery Mamie, and to witness the antics of the eastside maiden, chewing gum and resorting to all of the 'hick' vernacular imaginable, one could hardly believe that she and the stately blonde lady, so used to wooing high emotions, were one and the same. That Miss Lewis is thoroughly capable and competent in all of the ever-varying demands of stock is now quite definitely established.

Cliff Hastings made good again in a leading role and his popularity is seen at once by the applause in evidence at his every appearance. Mr. Hastings was breezy and buoyant as a sailor lad just in from the Philippines, where he had done all sorts of brave things in the service of Uncle Sam. From the rapidity and dispatch with which he felled to the floor diverse members of the company in the first and second acts, it must perforce be concluded that Jack Johnson has nothing on him, so why search further for a White Man's Hope?

The Others

The popularity which Miss Vickery is meriting was manifested in a friendly round of applause which marked her first appearance. Miss Vickery does the pretty heiress of the story with whom most of the Men of the cast, regardless of nationality, fall violently in love, taking up much of several acts with protestations of love which might well be taken note of by those considering taking similar incidents. Miss Vickery played the long and difficult role with consistency and balance, nor must the stunning gown worn by her in the second act be omitted in mention.

Mr. Merrill was uproariously entertaining as 'one of the finest' and Messrs. Garside and Ford lend much local color by their interpretation of denizens of the Chinese underworld. Miss Merschon as 'Crazy Kate' always assisted in this department of the entertain

ment. Mr. Merschon did a villainous heavy with much sinister maneuvering and his picture of a wicked Spanish gentlemen was most pronouncedly given.

It was sure a weird and rousing story and the audience fell for it with the whooping vengeance. The audience on Sunday night was an exceedingly large one and the success of the Garside's season seems entirely assured.

Monday's shows went exceedingly well, as did Tuesday's matinee. On Tuesday night, Olive arrived just in time for the show. I was so happy to see her and had so much I wanted to tell her.

At the last curtain call and after the introduction of the small orchestra, Garside took center stage addressing the audience. "Let's all give a hand to Miss Adella Lawton, one of Joplin's own, for her lovely piano accompaniment," he said, motioning for me to rise and take a bow. I stood there as pleased as I was stunned as the audience clapped. Then, the theater lights came up, and my moment of glory was over.

Olive came running over to me.

"Adella Lawton, you were wonderful. I am so proud of you," she gushed, throwing her arms around my neck and giving me a hug.

"Really? Did I do okay?"

"You did better than okay, Della. Is there someplace we can go and talk? Get caught up?"

"Maybe the soda shop is open. Do you want to go there?

"Not exactly what I had in mind," she said, giving me that look that Olive had whenever she was up to something. "Want to get a drink? I mean a real drink?

"Umm, I'm not sure about that tonight. Let's just go for a soda."

"Miss Lawton?" Jenkins came out of nowhere. "I do not believe that they need you for rehearsal tomorrow during the day. Please come down in the evening about six, okay? That should be the first dress rehearsal."

"I will," I said as he turned and left. The stagehands were busy getting everything around for the next performance, and I didn't see any performers.

I wanted to go out that back door to see if Cliff was having a cigarette. I wanted to talk to him more and learn about his life in Vaudeville. But the real reason that I wanted to see him, at least the reason I kept telling myself, was to find out if he realized that I was the girl he rescued at Joplin Creek.

Instead, Olive and I went back to my home for tea. She told me all about her trip to Kansas City, reminding me that we would be living there over the next few years. Olive wasted no time.

"Did you meet him?"

"Yes," I said, urging her to prod me further, which I enjoyed.

"Well, what was he like?"

"Amazingly gracious, not arrogant or condescending, and people love him. The women, they flock to him. But I can tell it has not all gone to his head like you would expect," I explained. "Near as I can tell, this whole troupe revolves around him and a few of the others. Of all of them, he is the most normal person you'd ever want to meet, very gentlemanly and patient to a fault. It's amazing how he tolerates the fans. Cliff has been very congenial with me. I am actually quite impressed by him."

"Cliff?" she repeated, as my face became flushed. I nodded in reply as Olive smiled.

"Does he remember you from the creek?"

"I really have no idea," I said, looking shyly away from her. "It never came up."

16

Actors feel rejection even when the audience adores them.

~CLIFFORD HASTINGS

When I arrived at rehearsal on Wednesday evening, I saw no one in the theater. There were empty chairs in a circle on the stage. On the top of my piano was a single red rose. The small note with it read, *"Thank you, Miss Lawton, for your smashingly good work. Cliff."*

"You really do not want to read too much into that." It was Elise, who was strolling up to the piano.

"I'm not reading anything into anything," I answered too quickly, crushing the note in my hand.

"You know that Cliff—he is a charmer," she said, fanning herself with a delicate white fan tied to her wrist.

"I guess he was just being thoughtful," I offered weakly. I really did not want to have this conversation with her.

"I'm not sure you understand about all this," she said, waving her finger around the room.

"Understand what?"

"How it works with men like Cliff."

"I still don't know what you mean," I said.

"Well, Cliff is a leading man in this company. Garside owns him so to speak, and there are rules that leading men must live by. They are forbidden to fool around with the help, or with anyone publicly. It's the image that they are trying to protect, Miss Lawton; the image of a single, handsome, available man. The ladies eat it up, and it keeps them all coming back for the shows. Garside would throw a fit if he saw you talking to Cliff, outside of a rehearsal, at least. It's in his contract."

So I was nothing but the "help." I had to set her straight. Now.

"You know, Miss Claredon, I really appreciate what you just said, but I think you have it all wrong. What you are insinuating is not true. There is nothing going on between me and Mr. Hastings."

"Lewis said she saw you two outside together."

"Oh, that was merely a coincidence. I happened to sneak out the back door of the theater and he happened to be there. I talked to him briefly. But let me set you straight. I'm a musician, not an actress and certainly not some doting fan of Mr. Hastings. I am here to perform and not to chase actors. I cannot help what you or Miss Lewis might think you saw. The fact that Mr. Hastings left me a note I am sure is only him thanking me for my work. And in my opinion, this place could use a bit more of his type of gratitude and thoughtfulness." As the words tumbled out of me, I could feel myself getting more visibly upset.

"Well, I really did not mean to upset you, Miss Lawton. I am sorry if I did. I'm not suggesting that you're having a scandalous affair with him. I think it is real important for you to know that there are boundaries here to which you must abide."

A scandalous affair? "Yes, well, you may consider me warned."

"It's not a warning, honey, just information. You know, you are a real, nice, talented, young girl. You don't want to throw all that away by getting yourself into a bad situation with an older man. You know performers move around a lot. They have no one to answer to, and they will not hesitate to take an innocent girl like you someplace where you don't want to go."

"You sure don't need to worry about me. Are you here to rehearse?"

"No, I'm not in this next play, and I guess we're not doing specialties with this one. See you around though." She turned and walked slowly across the stage and disappeared behind the curtain.

Garside walked out onto the stage as if perfectly on cue. "Good evening, Miss Lawton."

I never had a good feeling about Garside. Maybe it was his turn to pick on me.

"Mr. Garside, I understand that I am not here to rehearse specialties?'

"No, Miss Lawton. We are going to try something different. Have you ever seen films on a Kinodrome?"

"Yes, in other Vaudeville shows."

"Well, I have a friend passing through who has a Kinodrome show, and we're going to show that between acts. He has some shorter films. What do you think?" he asked matter-of-factly.

"It might be interesting. I know people are intrigued by the silent films. On the other hand, the specialties performers do a real nice job," I said, trying to be diplomatic.

"You watch, the Kinodrome will be a big hit, something different for these folks to see." He turned away. "Hey, Vic, you guys ready to go?"

Vic and Cliff walked in and sat down, and an older lady that I had not seen before joined them.

Garside whispered to me, "That's Emma Warren. You may have heard of her. She is a wonderful actress."

"Oh, yes," I said, nodding in agreement as I stared at a total stranger that I had never heard of before.

Opening night of this show came and went to a packed audience without a glitch. The Kinodrome shows played between acts, and the audience was enthralled by the Garside show. Afterward, Pete, the stagehand who had escorted me home before, showed up to escort me safely home.

The newspaper described the show perfectly:

Garside Stock Company Opens to Packed House
Present: "The Devil's Kitchen"
Melodrama Makes Biggest
Kind of Hit with the Patrons of the Theatre

At the theatre last night the Garside Stock Company gave a very interesting demonstration of just how artistically, melodrama—really, truly, no getting away from it, melodrama can be handled by a company of capable people.

Their means of demonstration was 'The Devil's Kitchen,' a top-notch thriller of the first water, and from the way the vast audience took it, there was no gainsaying the fact that it pleased mightily. There wasn't an empty seat in the place by the time the curtain arose, the house having been one of the best of the season.

Plenty of Mystery

The average theatre-goer ordinarily sits up and spoofs at a melodrama; Even if he enjoys it, he's afraid to say so for fear his neighbor will think his tastes are degenerating. But the crowd at the theatre last night evidently were not of that stripe for they manifested their enjoyment of the play in an unmistakable manner throughout the entire course. There's an element of mystery about the thing that kind o' gets you and holds you gripped, regardless of the 101 little tricks of melodrama that have been done to death by the 'rip and tear' troupes from time immemorial.

Harry Vickery does a piece of work as the Shadow which is way in the lead of any stock actor that has played this Season. The characterization—that of a man leading a dual life—is a difficult one.

Cliff Hastings, the young leading man, deserves notice right up near the top, he never failed to meet every situation, and came off with flying colors as the Detective. Emma Warren, shrouded in black, did a serious heavy. She acquitted herself finely and added a dignity and care which added much to the credit of the performance last night.

And Eugene Merrill put on a fine performance as the colored butler.

It didn't occur to me at the time that it was odd to have a colored butler played by a white man instead of a colored. This was the way it was because the colored performers had their own minstrel shows and kept to their own kind.

When I showed up early for the Monday matinee performance, Cliff and Vic were on the stage anxiously reading through the newspaper review.

"So how does it feel, Vic, to finally get top billing from these blokes?" inquired Cliff, reading over his shoulder. "Don't let it go to your head too much chap 'cause they'll have you back on your bum in no time."

"You know...this is good, real good," Vic said as he read. "It's about time they recognized who really has all the talent around here."

"Yes, yes, old chap, you do a great job playing a villain, or were you just being yourself?" Cliff bandied back. "I'm not sure they would love you as much as a lover boy."

"Careful," Vic said. "Don't you go insulting my manliness, too, Cliff."

"Hello, Miss Lawton," Cliff said, spotting me as I sat down at the piano. "Just enjoying the few pat on the back sides that we get from your newspaper here."

"I prefer the English word 'bum,'" Vic said, not taking his eyes from the newspaper.

Cliff sat down on the piano bench next to me. "It's a known fact, actors feel rejection even when the audience adores them...we thrive on it, that why he's up there voraciously reading the news."

"Yes, well, it was a good review, which means you should have a pretty good crowd tonight and for the rest of this show," I offered without looking at Cliff, though I was a bit nervous about even talking to these performers about anything not related to my piano work for fear that the wrong person might get the wrong impression. So I continued to shuffle through my music.

"That reminds me," Cliff said. "I am going to need an hour of your time on Wednesday morning to rehearse a song for the next show. Can you come around nine?"

"Garside is letting you do specialties again?" I blurted out.

"Now that his bloody Kinodrome friend has moved on to Texas," answered Vic imitating Cliff, not looking up from the page.

Cliff chuckled, "But it's just jolly old me this time doing the specialties...no one else."

No one else as in my friend, Miss Claredon, I thought.

"Mr. Hastings?" I said. "What do you have against showing off the Kinodrome?"

"Oh, don't get him started," chimed Vic. "We don't have all day."

"He's right at that, Miss Lawton. It would take a bit for me to explain."

"More like several days," Vic added.

"But I'd love to explain it to you sometime," Cliff said with a smile. "So will I see you then on Wednesday at nine?"

"I'll be there, unless Mr. Jenkins says I cannot for some reason."

"Fabulous!" he said. Cliff and Vic, with paper in hand, strolled off disappearing from view at back of the stage. It was time to get ready for the next show.

I noticed there was a sealed envelope on the top of my piano, next to a fresh red rose. The envelope was addressed to "Miss Lawton." *Dear Miss Lawton:* the note read.

I thought it would be a good idea to give you a copy of the rules of the Club Theater. If I have already given you these, here is a second copy for your files. Please make sure you read and abide by all of the rules. Sincerely, Mr. Jenkins.

Attached to the note was a list entitled, "Rules of the Club Theater Establishment." It read: *All employees of the Club Theater shall abide by the following rules:* Rule No. 5 had been underlined. *No fraternizing with Theater guests or customers, including performers.*

I could feel my Irish temper start to flare. I had not been fraternizing with anyone. This had to be the work of Elise or Marion, who must have said something about my chance meeting with Cliff. I felt like screaming, "You've got it all wrong!" Maybe I would scream later, but not here and now. I folded the note back up and put it back in the envelope. My hand was shaking. It's a good thing no one was here yet. I wondered whether I should immediately go to Mr. Jenkins and explain. No, not now, a voice said in my head.

Who I talk to and when was my business and no one else's! I wished Olive was there to give me advice. I reached in my case to look for some music. I needed to find something that would soothe and relax me. I found Chopin's "Etude in E Tristesse Opus 10 No. 3," which I had been working on in recent days. I sat there alone and played this beautiful piece, losing myself in the music as it filled the room. I went right into Chopin's "Piano Concerto No. 1 in E Minor."

When I finished, I heard a burst of applause. Turning, I saw a small audience in the back of the theater. It was Cliff, Vic, Merrill, and Ford, who were all walking toward me while applauding.

"Bravo!" said Cliff. "I could listen to you all day, everyday."

"You like Chopin?" I said, as our eyes met.

"We all do," Vic said. "You play it beautifully."

I turned to look at Vic. "Thank you."

"You're not the typical piano player—that is for sure," Merrill said.

"You are an amazing young girl," Cliff said under his breath.

"I have studied a long time. I'm not used to your blandishments," was all I could say to them as my face turned red.

"Will you play something else?" Ford said.

"I will play you one more song. This is Chopin's 'Nocturne No. 2 in E flat Opus 9 No. 2.'" They took their seats in the front row to listen. This was the first time I had actually seen these men stop working long enough to relax.

17

The stage is not merely the meeting place of all of the arts,
but is also the return of art to life.

~OSCAR WILDE (1854-1900)

It was already Wednesday morning. The company had concluded the last night of *The Devil's Kitchen,* and the town loved the melodrama. I was feeling exhausted. Two more plays to go, and then I hoped I would have a break. I really wanted to plan a trip with Olive to Kansas City for a couple weeks to see the city and do some shopping. If I was going to be a classy musician, I needed to be more glamorous and wear fashionable dresses and hats, the kind you couldn't buy in Joplin, Missouri.

Jenkins told me to show up for rehearsal at nine o'clock sharp. Cliff was waiting for me at the piano when I walked into the theater.

"Hi there, little Miss Sunshine," he said. "Are you ready to go?"

"I'm exhausted," I said. "When do you ever take a break?"

"It's called unemployment. That's when I take a break," he said seriously, but with a glimmer of humor in his eye.

"How do you do this day after day, night after night?" I asked.

Cliff thought a moment. "Actually, I think it has much to do with the fact that I love what I do. We all love what we do. It's not about fame or money. Don't get me wrong—we all do this for the money. But it's also about touching people's lives by bringing live theater to the people in all the towns that we visit. You can't do that with moving pictures, you know.

"For most of these people, they would never, ever have the chance to go to New York or Boston to see a show, much less afford the ticket for a show there. I, for one, do not want to be in New York or Boston. I've been there. It's not gratifying for me to perform in a city like Boston, night after night, year after year. The system is much more sullied there, and as a performer, we have so much more control over our work and the money we make out here. The audience back east is different, too…let's just say they're a bit more sophisticated and expect a much more elaborate show. They would never enjoy what we do. People out here, well, they love what we do for them. We make them smile or cry depending upon the show. We give them a different view of life, or we take them away from the harsh reality of life for some short bit. Out here on the plains of America, you don't have to have the highest paid actors or the most expensive sets or the most glorious costumes," he said as if he was dreaming.

"You don't have to deal with the Syndicate controlling your every move. There's a bureaucracy here, don't get me wrong, but it isn't anything like the Syndicate. They control everything back east.

"The actors are different, too. Look at Harry, for instance…he is the salt of the earth. He would do anything for me and I, for him. Most of us do not have enormous egos that have to be constantly nurtured. We work well together. We're a team. We want each of us to do well. We don't have to try and outperform each other or the theater up the street.

"People out here in the heartland of America truly appreciate what we do and they love letting us tell them a story. You should read the letters that I get from people showing their appreciation. That is why I do this day after day and night after night."

I was almost in a trance listening to him speak. I felt that I could listen to him all day. When he stopped talking, it took me a minute to realize it.

"You are admirable—I give you that," I said. "And I understand what you mean. I really do because I have similar feelings about my music."

"Do you ever think about joining a company?" he asked.

"I have thought about it, but I need to get some more schooling before I go do something like that. Anyways, I'm still pretty young, and I know right now my parents would not like it too well if I took up the life of Vaudeville." I wanted to hear more about him. "What was Boston like?"

"Boston...hmm. I have good and bad memories of Boston. It was my first home in the United States, technically Medford. At first, I felt a bit lost. No friends or family there, no job and not many prospects of getting a job, at least a job that I liked. I worked as a machinist for a while. Then I met people who knew people in the theater, and here I am. But don't think for a minute that I started where I am today. This business has a way of keeping a sane man ever so humble. No, I started as a theater ticket taker, then an usher, and then I worked my way up to doing set work. Actually, I would strike the set when the play was done." He smiled to himself.

"My first real contract was as a stage carpenter, and I made $25.00 a week. Lucky for me I knew how to use a hammer, and I wasn't afraid of getting my hands dirty. Then I met some people who helped me get started in Vaudeville, singing. I've worked with so many Vaudeville and stock companies, and I found Vaudeville performers to be most interesting and quite fun to be around. From Vaudeville, I started getting theater gigs in stock companies.

"I've been able to see so much of America and touch so many people's lives. In 1910, I signed on to do several plays with the George Amusement Company at the Warrington Theater in Oak Park, Illinois. The further west I came, the more opportunity there was to do what I really wanted to do, and the Syndicate doesn't have quite the stranglehold on all of the theaters out here that it has in the east. I gave it a go with Gilson & Bradford. Then I went over to the Morey Stock Company in El Dorado, Texas. We did shows like *Dixie Land, Sweet Clover,* and *The End of the Trail.* I was in Hibbing, Minnesota, in the summer of 1910 at the Healy Theater with the Fisher Stock Company. We did shows like, *The Heir to the Hoorah, The Little Minister*, and *The Belle of Richmond.* I've worked with wonderful performers, Anna Brandt, Mae O'Reilly, Theresa Martin, Harry LaCour, Boyd Trousdale, Mae McCaskey, Earl Howell, Charles Burnham, and many, many more.

"But none of them come close to how I feel about the performers that I am with now, Vic, Marion, Fred, Gene. We found each other in Vaudeville performing as the Alpha Quintet. Now we are having pretty decent success together in stock theater. I am not sure where this troupe is headed, but

I hope we can keep our core group together, at least for a bit longer," he paused for a moment.

"Well, enough of my dribbling on. I really do need you to help me with this new song so I don't sound like a blubberin' fool out there." He handed me a new sheet of music.

"Of course," I said politely.

We rehearsed the song twice, and he sang it beautifully both times. When he was done, Cliff graciously thanked me for my time.

"Miss Lawton?"

"Yes."

"Have you ever heard of Rachmaninov?"

"No, I haven't."

"I will see that you get some of his music. He is a favorite composer of mine." He started to walk away and then turned back to look at me, his eyes not quite reaching mine. "Miss Lawton, we are having a picnic lunch on Sunday. You are welcome to join us," he offered.

"Oh, no thank you, Cliff. Really, I have other plans on Sunday. I appreciate that you thought to invite me," I said, as there was no way I was going anywhere near this man outside of this theater.

Cliff looked at me for a moment as if he wanted to say something more. As his solemn expression changed into a smile, he nodded his head and left me to join the other actors on the stage.

The next week passed quickly, mainly because the shows were well received. Garside allowed Cliff to perform specialties for each show, charming the women with his ways. They loved him for it.

I felt sad to see this time come to an end. Even though I had only spent two weeks with these performers, I felt like I was part of them in some way, especially one particular performer.

The company was all packed up and gone by Sunday morning. They disappeared by train as quickly as they appeared. I think I heard that they were going on to Iowa.

After church on Sunday, I stopped by the theater to practice some new music that I was working on. The theater was quiet, dark, and empty. On the top of the piano were a single red rose and a card addressed to me. It read, *On behalf of the Garside Stock Company, we all wish to thank you for your beautiful piano accompaniment.* Everyone had signed the card, even Miss Claredon. On the back of the card was a note in the most beautiful handwriting. *Miss Lawton: I hope we will meet again someday. Until then, best of luck with your music lessons. I have truly enjoyed your fantastic talent! By the way, I want you to know that I now know you were the girl at Joplin Creek. I hope you' will forgive me for not realizing it sooner. Forever truly yours, Clifford Hastings.*

18

Minerva House was a finishing establishment for young ladies where some twenty girls of the ages from thirteen to nineteen, inclusive, acquired a smattering of everything and knowledge of nothing.

~CHARLES DICKENS (1812–1870)

My summer working at the Club Theater seemed to pass quickly after the Garside Stock Company left town. I enjoyed my time at the theater playing the piano. There were several more Vaudeville shows that came through, another theatrical touring company, a few wedding receptions, and several formal dinners where I entertained the guests playing piano for most of the dinner hour.

There were a couple of boys that came around that summer to see Olive and me. Of course, Albert accompanied me to the Jasper County Fair, but we had very little time together because I always worked in the evenings at the Club and he worked in his father's law office as a clerk during the day. It was no secret to me that Albert wanted to practice law with his father, settle down in Joplin, and get married to a wife who stayed home all day and raised up a bunch of his kids. Albert was the essence of stability, a real family man. I was quite fond of him, but I think Mama and Papa liked him the best. Even so, they had other plans for me.

Olive's mother had talked Mama and Papa into sending me with Olive to finishing school in Kansas City. The school we planned to attend had actually burned to the ground during the winter of 1913. What was left of the school merged with another school, and the finishing course work was offered in a new location.

As Olive's mother had explained, in finishing school we would learn to be polite and courteous, talk in appropriate sentences, walk without slouching, set a formal dinner table, write thank you notes, dress, wear corsets, make corsets tighter, style our hair, paint our faces, be good wives, and run households like "ladies." The school also had a music curriculum where I could continue my piano studies.

Around the end of July, I received a box of sheet music in the mail from a music store in St. Louis. There was music of Rachmaninov, Brahms, DeBussy, and other composers that I had never heard of. Cliff had sent the box of music, without a return address, just a card that said, "Enjoy."

The following week I received a subscription to *Etude* magazine in the mail, which was a monthly magazine with everything about music you can imagine. There were lessons with pages of new sheet music and advertisements about every music school in the country. It must have been from Cliff, but there was not even a card with this gift.

On my last day at the Club, Mr. Jenkins, who usually was devoid of emotion, actually seemed sad to see me go. "You make sure you come back and see us, Miss Lawton," he said as he handed me a small card. In the card was a season's pass to the plays at the Club. It was thoughtful, but I had no idea when I would use it.

"How very thoughtful of you, Mr. Jenkins." I did not have the heart to tell him that I had no plans to return to Joplin anytime soon.

Emily came around her desk and handed me a small package wrapped in pink and white paper. It was a beautiful china teacup with gold trim, and it had the quaintest gold-trimmed pink and white saucer to match.

"I bought this in Paris when I was there. I couldn't think of a more fitting gift for you, now that you are going off to finishing school to learn to become a lady," Emily said.

"This is beautiful, Emily. I will always treasure it." As I hugged Emily for the first and last time, I knew this china teacup would never see any tea;

no, it would be displayed in the dish cupboard for all to admire. And so I began collecting china teacups from the places that I visited.

After Labor Day, 1914, Albert and I parted ways. He went off to study law with his uncle's firm in St. Louis, and Olive and I took a train up to finishing school in Kansas City. At the Union Depot, Albert kissed me good-bye on the lips. I wasn't sure if I wanted to be kissed by him, so I was a bit hesitant. It might have been an awkward moment but for the fact that it happened so fast. Before he walked away, he squeezed my hand and promised to write me often.

19

America is too proud to fight.
~PRESIDENT WOODROW WILSON (1856–1924)

On June 28, 1914, the Arch Duke Fran Ferdinand of Austria was assassinated. Austria-Hungary believed that Serbia was behind the assassination and sent an ultimatum to Serbia. Before long, Germany sided with Austria-Hungary, and Russia sided with Serbia. In a very short time, most of Europe's major powers were at war. I never quite understood how this one event in a land so far away from my own could lead to World War I.

Thanks to President Wilson, the United States stayed out of the war for almost three years, but one thing led to another, and on April 6, 1917, the Congress and President Wilson officially declared war on Germany, which I thought was the beginning of the end of the life I had come to love.

In the late spring of 1915, I received a handwritten letter from Mama explaining to me in her quiet way all of the reasons why she thought I should come home. It came down to the fact that with the war overseas and the possibility of the country getting involved in the war, Mama wanted me home. It was the sinking of the British luxury liner, *Lusitania* in May,

1915, by the Germans and the senseless death of over one thousand civilians, some of whom were Americans, that caused Mama to write me again, almost begging me to come home. It was clear she hadn't been this upset since the *Titanic* sunk in 1912, so she insisted that I could get my job back at the Club in September because Mr. Jenkins had inquired about me.

Her letters took me by surprise, not because Mama was asking me to come home, but because I really did not want to go back to Joplin. I had changed immensely in the year that I had been away. I was no longer a naive little Joplin girl in handmade cotton frocks. I had been to finishing school and had a part time job in Kansas City giving piano lessons. I made good money and was well respected by the parents whose children I taught. Sometimes I even played the piano for the choir of the Episcopal Church in Kansas City. Olive, who was busy getting her school teacher's certificate, wanted to be a high school English literature teacher.

Olive and I dated a few young men from the local boy's college, but neither one of us felt real love for a man yet. Olive was still writing letters to Jake, who had gone off and joined the U.S. Army because all he wanted to do was fight in the war.

And Albert—well, I stopped writing to Albert after a few months. I guess we mutually agreed to go our own way with the slim hope that someday maybe our paths would cross again. Even so, I had no idea what to expect when they did. Most of the folks who knew me were expecting me to settle down with Albert because he was a good catch for a girl from Joplin.

I had grown accustomed to Kansas City and all of the advantages of a bigger city. Aside from all of the educated, interesting people, there were wonderful clothing shops, music stores, and bookstores. There were great restaurants, art fairs, and festivals. Live theater and Vaudeville shows came through Kansas City regularly. There seemed to be more art and culture, and I was definitely enjoying all of it. I often thought of Cliff when I was at the theater. I still felt drawn to him, although I did not see him while I was in Kansas City and never expected to see him again. But I tried to keep track of his whereabouts by collecting newspaper articles about him. One article that I saved in my scrapbook came from a roommate from Iowa.

> *J.S. Garside opened his third season of Spring and Summer Stock at Dubuque, IA, May 13, with his own show. After the opening show the company gave a banquet to Clifford Hastings the leading man, in honor of the anniversary of his birth, and presented him with a beautiful ruby ring and stickpin to match. The presentation was made by Marion Lewis, the leading woman of the company. The Company spent most of the past winter in the south, being 18 weeks in Paducah, KY where they broke all records for business. They have been together now for thirty-five weeks without a break in ranks. Two bills a week will be put on through the summer at Dubuque.*

Another article from her read:

> *Cliff Hastings left the Garside Stock Company at Dubuque, Iowa, July 6 and joined the Van Dyke and Eaton Stock Co., at Des Moines the following night, to play opposite leads to Bessie Jackson.*
>
> *A peculiar feature of the engagement is that the one whose place Mr. Hastings filled with the Van Dyke and Eaton Co., succeeded him with the Garside Co.*

I was surprised that he left Garside's troupe because he was so fond of the performers. But Cliff did not stay in one place too long, or as Papa would say, "no grass grew under his feet." I was happy to see that he had found a way to move on in his career.

Olive made it known to everyone that I had a crush on an actor. On a few occasions, she would even drop his name in public. *"Yes, I know him. I played the piano for him once,"* I would say. The older women were awestruck. They didn't even know Cliff Hastings, but for the seemingly romantic characters he played on stage. Most would probably not even recognize him if they saw him on the street. They didn't know him like I knew him. Cliff and I had a special connection, at least I thought so, and I think he did as well because of the way he signed his name on that last note he wrote to me, *"Forever truly yours."* When I thought of him, which was often, I remembered his carefully chosen words.

Still, I couldn't help but wonder if Miss Lewis or Miss Claredon were still with him and if he had settled down in other ways. If he had, no one would know it because they would never let it be known. That's the way it was in his world, according to Miss Elise Claredon. For all I knew, Miss Marion Lewis could be his wife by now, or maybe Bessie Jackson. Who was I kidding—he and I—we never had a chance and probably never will. He was way beyond me and not just in years.

20

Problem is our law wouldn't have protected Joe—not the way he needs to be protected. They know it and that's exactly why they bully people around. No, Joe might of ended up in peonage or worse.

~MICHAEL LAWTON

The possibility of war brought me home to Joplin, Missouri, on September 30, 1915. The Club Theater was still open for business although there were discussions about it closing in the future for remodeling. The theater patrons needed to raise the money first. Olive stayed in school up in Kansas City, working on her teaching certificate.

Papa and Mama met me at the train station. I hadn't seen my parents since the previous Christmas, so I was happy to see them and they were certainly happy to see me. Mama had tears in her eyes, and I was not sure if it was because she truly missed me or she was proud that I had blossomed into a grown up. She did not say.

There was a lot more than the possibility of war on their minds. The temperance movement was gaining more and more support to ban liquor across the country. So far, Missouri hung tight and didn't pass a bunch of local antiliquor ordinances like some of the other states. But each county would eventually have their say. If the temperance won out, Papa would lose the saloon. This battle with the do-gooder crusaders was bothering both of them. America was supposed to be the land of the free, and not the kind of place where the law told you what you could drink, he would say. Papa was growing tired of the hypocrisy. The politicians would make promises to the temperance crusaders during the day and spend their nights in a saloon drinking whiskey.

"Hey, Della, my girl," Papa said as he gave me a big hug and then loaded my luggage into the buggy. Papa still traveled by horse and buggy, even though many people were driving Ford Model Ts in Joplin. Olive and I were used to getting around in a taxicab in Kansas City.

"Hi, Papa," I said hugging him back. "Oh by the way, I go by the name Marie, now."

"Well, that's your middle name. It's a great name. It was my mother's name," Mama said as she reached for my hand.

"Do you two think you can get used to calling me Marie?"

"Sure, Della..." Papa chuckled.

"You look beautiful, child...I mean Marie, a very classy young lady. I love your suit," Mama said holding my face in her hands. I was dressed in a two-piece grey and pink tailored suit with a skirt that came to the middle of my calf. My large hat matched, and so did my gloves. Mama did not notice at first that my hair was shorter. "You have learned a lot in Kansas City?"

"Yes, I have truly enjoyed being there. I made a lot of new friends that I will truly miss. But I have missed you, too. And it will be good to spend some time here with you again." I hugged Mama. She looked tired and older.

"Did you meet any nice young men in Kansas City?" Papa asked. Mama gave him the evil eye for asking me that.

"I met a lot of nice young men. I taught them music lessons. They were twelve," I teased him. He looked at me oddly. "I met several men my age. I dated a few of them. But I was very busy with school and all, and the school really did not encourage us to date."

When I saw my parents for the first time after being away, why did the conversation revert to the men in my life? I had forgotten that I was expected to marry a stable man and start a family. It was also expected that I would stay at home and raise children while my husband had a career and provided for the family, and that I would give up the idea of playing the piano, except for church. What if I was not ready to give up my dreams? What if I was not ready to talk to them about men? I certainly did not want to tell them that only one man in this world interested me. If they knew who it was, they'd probably lock me away in an asylum. But sooner or later, it slipped out.

"Albert was home this past summer. He worked for his dad," Mama said. "He asked about you."

"He did?" I was surprised. "It was Albert's idea that we stop writing to each other. I had thought that he had met someone."

"It doesn't sound like he broke your heart too much," Papa said.

"No, there's only one man that could do that," I mumbled under my breath, but they both heard it and looked at me.

"I'm not talking with you about this," I said. "Please, just never mind."

I quickly changed the subject. "Tell me, is Mr. Jenkins expecting me?"

"He told me to tell you to take a week or so and rest up, get to know the town again. Then come down and see him," said Papa, patting me on the shoulder.

That was exactly what I did because the train ride from Kansas City was exhausting. The first night, I probably slept for two nights straight through. Mama cooked and brought me breakfast in bed. She cleaned and pressed my clothes and pampered me as much as I would let her. Aunt Maggie fussed over me, too, and Uncle Sam offered to take me anywhere I wanted to go in the buggy.

On Sunday afternoon, we had a family dinner like we did in the old days. Mama made roast goose with apple and walnut stuffing. Aunt Maggie made pecan pie for dessert. After dinner, Mama was busy in the kitchen. Aunt Maggie and Uncle Sam took a walk. Papa and I had a chance to talk.

"You know, Marie, I don't know if I ever told you this before...can't really remember tellin' ya, don't really reckon whether I did or not..."

"Tell me what?" Papa was too busy smoking his pipe.

"Remember that theater group that was here last summer after you graduated? Don't remember the name."

"You mean the Garside Stock Company?"

"Yeah, the one with that English fellow in it."

"Yes," I said slowly. I could feel my heart beating faster.

"Well, they came into the saloon the night 'fore they left town."

"Oh really?"

He was talking so slowly.

"And the English fellow and the one named Vic were together, and they recognized me as being the guy they helped out of that scrape I was having at the creek. And we got to talkin'...I mentioned that you was my daughter, the one that was involved. They were both pretty surprised 'cause you been workin' down there at the Club and all. I guess neither one of them had a clue that you was the gal they rescued."

"You told them it was me?"

"Yeah, was I s'posed to keep it a secret?"

"Oh no, I just never realized how they found out."

"You knew that they knew?" he asked.

"Sort of, but not until the note," I said. "One of them left me a thank you note that told me that he *knew I was the girl by the creek*." Papa was silent.

"Papa, why did those men attack you that day?"

He shrugged. "Not sure you want to know the answer to that."

"I'm a big girl. Tell me."

After a long pause, Papa said, "I expect it was a group of very bad men, and I had a colored man workin' for me. They didn't like that. They were threatening to kill Joe if he didn't work the fields. Lynch 'em. They tried to claim Joe trespassed on their land; Joe never been to their land. So I got McGinnis involved to investigate, and they got mad...at me."

"Kill Joe? Why on earth would they want to kill Joe? He never did anything wrong."

"That's what they do. They said that I should only have white men workin' in my saloon. They just wanted Joe for themselves."

"I had no idea. Are there more people like that?"

"They're all over. Most of them hide behind hoods or masks and do their dirty work that way. Some say they been lynching colored people all over Missoura. When it comes right down to it though, they's cowards, not brave enough to fight fair. They's got to fight in groups with their face covered, afraid to go one on one like a man."

"Lynch Joe? This is just crazy thinking! They all need to be stopped... put away...jail or something worse."

"Easier said than done." He shook his head. "They think they got the right because of the law being separate but equal. Problem is our law wouldn't have protected Joe—not the way he needs to be protected. They know it and that's exactly why they bully people around. No, Joe might of ended up in peonage or worse.

I didn't know what he was talking about. "Peonage?"

"Slavery. It works like this, an unsuspecting, black man is charged with a crime that he didn't commit, and the only way he can get out of it is to work it off for a white man, for next to nothin'. Three plantation owners in Missoura have already gone to trial. The feds are starting to get wise to this ploy."

"What about the law?"

"It's a damn crooked law enforced by crooked men and they have no intention of protectin' men like Joe, and every intention of takin' advantage of his plight. But the law would protect me for protecting Joe and our McGinnis is a straight shooter. That they did not count on."

I couldn't believe what he was telling me.

"Anyway, I wanted you to know that I had a grand old time with those actors. They's pretty funny guys. But they had no clue you were the little girl that they rescued, no clue at all," he said, chuckling to himself.

"I hope you bought them a drink," I said. "You owed them that much."

"Yeah, I bought them a few. What they did was all right by me, pretty talented guys to pull off that stunt. The English guy seemed to have a thing for you."

"What do you mean?"

"The way he talked about you and your talent…I told him he better stay away."

"Papa, you didn't. Did you?"

"Not in so many words. But neither your mother nor I want you running off with a traveling actor. That's no kind of life for you. You need to find yourself a nice, stable boy, settle down in one place and raise a family. You wouldn't have to give up your music. You can teach piano lessons to kids…maybe get a job with the school."

"What if that is not what I want right now?"

"What do you think you want?" Mama asked as she came into the living room.

"I'm not real sure, but I enjoyed the city, and I want to see more places, meet more people. I might want to perform on some level, not just teach.

I'm not ready to settle down in one place, but I'm not sure that I have much of an option."

"Why do you say that?" Mama asked.

"Well, Olive's still in school, and I'm not about to just take off by myself and travel. The world's not a safe place for a woman traveling alone. So for now, I guess you are stuck with me, unless I go back to Kansas City."

"We might not be here for long either," Papa said. "The temperance is getting stronger. It'll be no time 'fore liquor is banned if they have it their way."

Joplin had changed some in the time that I had been gone. There were more buildings, stores, factories, and people. Women were allowed in some of the saloons, even the Criterion. Papa worked every night of the week, even Sunday night. Mama often went to work with him and helped out washing the glasses and serving the customers. The telegraph had finally come to Joplin. There was a telegraph station uptown, and women were trained to work as telegraph operators. Being a telegraph operator might be an interesting job, but it took training that I did not have, nor much want.

21

*Life is like playing the violin in public and learning the
instrument as one goes on.*
~**SAMUEL BUTLER (1835-1902)**

I went to see Jenkins after resting for a week. Even though he still could
not outwardly show his emotion, he seemed eager to get me back to work
for the fall season. He told me about the wedding receptions and Vaudeville
traveling shows coming to the Club before Christmas. Jenkins booked
dinners every Friday night at the Club for different local groups. A local
restaurant usually catered and served the food while I played piano music
through the dinner hour. Once in a while he lined up a barbershop quartet
to sing before the dinner hour.

There were more women than men these days in Joplin. Many of the
young men had joined the army because most folks thought that was the
right thing to do, and the mass exodus of young men going off to war
opened up even more good jobs for women in Joplin.

Albert showed up at the theater one Friday night in early December.
He was accompanied by woman, a pretty brunette. Maybe that was why he
acted real surprised to see me when I walked up to his table.

"Hello, Albert, so good to see you." I touched his arm, as I wondered whether he was the same person I used to adore.

"Adella," he said "I had heard a rumor you were back in town. This is Susan Fields," he said, introducing me to his date. "This is Adella Lawton. She's the entertainment here."

"A pleasure to meet your acquaintance, Adella," she said as she shook my hand ever so delicately. "I believe we have met before. We were in high school at the same time. I am a year younger than you," Susan offered as she glanced at Albert.

Albert appeared to be gloating.

"Oh sure," I nodded. "I think I do remember you."

"Susan is a legal secretary in my father's office," Albert said.

"I bet that is an interesting job," I said to her. She nodded in agreement.

"Albert, are you close to being a lawyer?" I asked.

"Do you have to ask?" he said. "I'm reading the law and working under my father now. It comes natural to me."

"Is it difficult?"

"Not for me."

"Oh," I said.

The silence was deafening. "Well, good luck with your studies...I must get back to my piano. It was nice to meet you, Susan, and to see you again, Albert." I turned on one foot and walked away, not quite sure how I was feeling. Albert and I had been such close friends, and now everything was so formal again as if nothing we ever said or did actually meant anything. He was condescending and had the arrogance of a typical lawyer, someone who thought he knew everything and could do anything. He had become a stranger to me, and it felt real awkward. It wasn't sadness or happiness that I felt; it was numbness, I guess. Susan seemed nice and pretty, and she likely would make a good wife for the boy that Mama and Papa had picked out for me.

I did not hear from Albert after that meeting, but his engagement to Miss Susan Fields was announced in the newspaper soon after.

22

Happiness-not in another place, but this place...,
not for another hour, but this hour.
~WALT WHITMAN (1819-1892)

The fall passed quickly and pretty soon the holidays were here. Several holiday parties were held at the Club, and I was often the main attraction, along with Santa Claus, who would always make an appearance to get everyone in the Christmas spirit. I was making good money at this point and had accumulated a nice savings account of my own. I thought of it as part of my Hope Chest, which was supposed to consist of everything that I would need if ever I was married.

Christmas Eve at the Club was always an event. Many of the townspeople filled the theater to wish each other a Merry Christmas. There was singing and dancing and plenty of good food, whiskey, and champagne. I played the piano jubilantly while people gathered around and sang Christmas carols. Someone gave me a glass of champagne, and before you know it, I had three glasses of champagne. I think it actually helped me to relax and play Christmas carols for the joyful crowd of patrons who were hovering like bees on honey around the piano singing their hearts out. I took a break about ten. It had grown stuffy in the Club, and I felt like I needed some air.

As I was walking to the front door of the theater, a tall well-dressed gentleman came through the door with a crowd of people.

Our eyes met. "Miss Lawton," Cliff said as if he was happy to see me.

"Mr. Hastings," I said breathlessly as I walked toward him reaching out with both hands as if to catch him. The crowd of women heard me say his name and looked toward Cliff.

"Is that Cliff Hastings?" I heard one of them say as the crowd moved toward him.

"It looks like him," another one said as she started walking his way.

He grabbed my hand and pulled me vigorously through a side door at the theater entrance that was a hallway to the back of the stage area. Cliff looked quite handsome in his suit and he was wearing the ruby stickpin from Bessie Jackson on the lapel of his suit coat.

"Come with me. I want to talk to you." The door shut behind us, and he fumbled to turn the lock.

"I only have a minute before I have to play again." My heart started to race.

"I'll wait for you."

"What are you doing here?" I was not only surprised but totally bewildered by his presence.

"I'm on a bit of a break. We start the winter season here in Joplin after New Years."

"You'll be here?" I was dizzy from the champagne. I stumbled, and Cliff caught my arm.

"Are you okay?" he chuckled. He seemed delighted that I had a little too much champagne and was likely making a fool of myself stumbling around.

"I'm okay, I think...I had champagne, probably too much." I could feel the blood rush to my cheeks. My face was warm. As I leaned against the wall, I thought it was the champagne making me dizzy, but it occurred to me that it might have been the fact that he had come to Joplin early just to see me, or so I wanted to believe.

"Why, of all places, did you come here now?" I said.

He smiled his wonderful smile and met my glance. "I couldn't think of any other place I wanted to be or person I wanted to see on Christmas Eve."

This did not make any sense to me.

"Did you get the music and the magazine?"

"I did, thank you." We stood there quietly looking at one another.

"I haven't heard from you since you left town a year and a half ago, and I'm to believe that you came here to see me?"

"Honestly, I've come back to see you two or three times, but you were gone," he said defensively.

"But why now?"

"Why not now? I have some free time, which is rare as you well know." He reached up and gently touched my face. I'm sure I blushed. "You look absolutely stunning," he quietly said.

I looked at him in disbelief. "I really have to get back to the piano." I started walking away. What was I doing? I quickly turned back to him.

"Will you come with me?" I stumbled, and he caught my arm again.

"I will, if you promise not to say my name to anyone."

"I promise."

"No announcements or introductions. Not even to Jenkins."

"None," I agreed as I pretended to zip my mouth shut with my hand. "You should follow me, but come out separately." I instructed as he squeezed my hand and then let go.

In a fog, I walked from the backstage to the piano alone, sat down and opened with "Hark the Herald Angels Sing." A crowd of carolers formed around me. Other people continued to huddle in small groups around the room. Cliff blended in with the crowd at the piano, and before I knew, he was singing along. His voice clearly carried the crowd. A waitress brought me another glass of champagne. It was then that it dawned on me that this was proving to be my best Christmas Eve ever.

When I started "Silent Night," Cliff sang it solo, and the rest of the people in the room crowded around us to hear him sing. When he was finished, there wasn't a dry eye in the group, and you could hear a pin drop. Out of a real fear that someone in this crowd would recognize him, I struck up "Jingle Bells," and the crowd broke into laughter and started singing again, only this time everybody sang along. Cliff really seemed to be enjoying himself and his brief moment of anonymity, just being part of the Christmas crowd. I did not want anything to happen to take that away from him. I finished my set playing one of my favorites, "Carol of the Bells," and everyone just listened.

When my last set was over, I took my bow on the stage and walked to the back of the stage into the darkness of a wing while the audience clapped and cheered. Now what? I thought. Then I felt someone take my hand in the darkness. Cliff pulled me to his chest and wrapped his arms around me. I felt so tiny next to him. I was so tiny next to him.

"That was wonderful, thank you," he whispered into my ear. Then with the slightest touch of his hand, he turned my head and gently kissed me. The champagne gave me the nerve I needed to kiss him back.

"I've been waiting a long time to do that." He looked at me. I could barely see his face because it was so dark at the back of the stage.

"I'm not sure what you mean by that," I whispered back. "And I'm not sure I even care. I've been waiting a long time to do this." I kissed him again, and having the freedom to kiss him, even on a dark stage, felt wonderful. Of course, when I thought about this moment later, I blamed it all on the champagne, because I never behaved this way with a man. When we were finished with the kiss, he held my face in his hands and stared at me in the dark.

"What do you want to do now?" he asked. "I'm up for anything you want. Are you hungry?"

I'd just as soon stay right here kissing you, I thought.

"Where are you staying?" I asked.

"The Connor, where I was before. Even have the same room, temporarily."

"Oh that won't do," I said. "Let me talk with my parents. Perhaps you could come over tomorrow?"

"It's Christmas tomorrow."

"Yes, we'll have a big dinner...we'll go to church in the morning. I have to sing in the choir and maybe, play the piano. Do you want to go?"

"That would be nice. Actually, it would be perfect."

"The service is at ten."

"Okay." He kissed my hair. He hesitated, "Is there someplace we can go now, just to talk?"

"There's a quaint little place up the street where we might be able to have a drink." I was not about to take him to the Criterion.

"Please, let's go there." He helped me with my coat, put his coat and hat on, and we left the theater through the back entrance. It was a windy night, and the wind was bitter cold for Joplin. We didn't get much snow in Joplin, but occasionally, when it was cold, it snowed. It was feeling like it was going to snow tonight. Cliff took my arm and escorted me, shielding me from the wind.

"How did you get here?" I asked.

"I have automobile. It's really Vic's Model T, but he let me use it."

"How is Vic?"

"Vic and Eunice are doing well, and Abby is doing very well."

"Eunice is Vic's wife? And Abby is their daughter?"

"Yes."

"I think I saw you with Abby at church?"

"Possibly, I can't even remember the last time I went to church."

When we were seated, he ordered more champagne for me and a brandy for himself.

"So, Cliff, what have you been doing, and what has happened to finally bring you back to Joplin?" I wanted to hear all about his travels.

"I'm with a new company, the Van Dyke and Eaton Company, and we have a lot of bookings over the next several months. Hell, we'll be here most of the winter season. But right now, we all needed a break...a break from the stage, a break from one another."

"I read about your new company. Who is in your group? Is Vic with you?"

"Here," he said as he reached in his pocket. "I've brought you a copy of a news release about us. It'll explain everything." He handed me a small crumpled piece of paper which read:

The New York Clipper. May 9.

Van Dyke and Eaton Co. Notes

Starting the first of May, coming, this company will enter its twenty-first year of success under the management of F. and C. Mack. During this period the company has played every city of any importance from the Ohio River and regions below to the Rocky Mountains, on the west, and the forty-ninth parallel on the North, and the Atlantic Seaboard on the East, and always with unvarying success...As it now stands this company has just closed an eight month engagement at the LaCrosse Theatre, LaCrosse, Wis. and has broken all records for length of

> *run and number of paid admissions in this city, having lost but one night since the 14 day of May. The company has a large repertoire of the very best and popular plays, producing such plays as "The Lion and the Mousse," "The Third Degree," "Paid-in-Full," "Beverly of Granstark," and plays of that class. Perhaps more remarkable still is the fact that there are with the company today members who have been with it for eleven years. The roster is F. and O. Mack, managers; Willard Foster, Whit Brandon, Clifford Hastings, W.E. LaRose, Harry Vickery, Everett White, Orrin T. Burke, Jack Boyle, Jimmy McCoy, Hugo Koch, M. Maranti, Lorena Tolsen, Eunice Elliott, Nantie St. Oyr, Chella Warner, Helen DeLand, Ethel Jane, Mary Enos, Helen Ried, Bessie Jackson, Wilma and Chase Gano.*

"There are so many more people in this company?" I remarked. "I see Harry and Eunice are still with you, but she goes by Eunice Elliott now."

"Rules," he said. "They're still very much married. At least the last time I saw them they were," he laughed.

"Why are you here now?"

"I am here now because..." he said to himself as if he was thinking out loud. "I have thought about you a lot over the last year. I really wanted to see you again."

"You barely talked to me when you were here."

"That is not so, is it?" He was struggling for words. "You cannot tell me that you do not feel it too," he said. "We have an attraction for each other. But you were way too young back then for me to act on it. That would not have been the proper thing for me to do. So I guess I am guilty of ignoring you back then, sort of, but not because I wanted to ignore you... but because I had to ignore you. You were a child."

"I had finished my schooling."

"You had *just* finished school, here. You were not more than sixteen. It would not have been proper for me to act on my desires." He changed the subject. "You have been away from Joplin?"

"Until September, I had been living in Kansas City. I went to school there. I took more music courses, piano. I loved my time there and I learned a lot." I did not want to tell him that I had been to a finishing school for women where I learned how to properly set tables and fold cloth napkins, but I think he could probably tell I was a little more refined than I used to be.

"You seem different, more grown up," he said. "What about your social life in Joplin? Do you have friends here still?"

"I am not currently dating anyone, if that's what you mean," I said. "Mama wanted me home because of the war, or else, I probably would still be in Kansas City with Olive."

"Is Olive your friend?"

"My best friend. She is getting a teaching certificate. Teaching will be a good career for her. I taught piano to school age children in Kansas City. It was a good job for me."

"You really have a performer's heart you know. I can tell that about you." I nodded in agreement. "So now is your time to figure out what you want out of life. Don't be afraid to go after what you want."

"If only that was true. It seems like society has predetermined my life." I was beginning to feel brave again because of the champagne. "You know, I have missed seeing you perform. You showed me something that I had never experienced—perhaps it was your independence, or maybe your confidence, but I had feelings for you that I had never felt before. Then a voice in my head told me I had to be dreaming. But here you are telling me I was not dreaming. You had feelings, too. What I felt for you may have been real, after all."

"I'm not a dream."

"You're not?"

"No, I am here and I am very real." Our eyes met for one very long minute. I was not comfortable continuing this conversation. It was way more intense than any conversation I was accustomed to having with a man.

"It's getting late. I probably need to get home, or my Papa will have half of Joplin out looking for me."

"I believe that. Let me take you home in the car." I stared at him not knowing what to say. "I promise I'll be a gentleman," Cliff offered.

We walked in the cool night to his car. He had his arm around my shoulders to keep me warm and away from the wind. In the car, he asked me if I was "cold." I told him "no." The truth was I was burning up inside. When we got to the alley behind the Criterion, he stopped the car, got out, and came around and opened my door. Papa was still in the saloon, but I'm sure Mama was upstairs waiting for me. As we walked to the door, he swung me around into his arms and gently kissed me again.

"Tonight was my best Christmas Eve in a long, long time," he whispered against my hair.

"Mine, too," I whispered back. "You will be here tomorrow?" I was afraid he was going to disappear into thin air like one of those dreams that you know you enjoyed, but you just can't remember.

"I will be here in the morning. We will go to church together and spend Christmas together if that's what you wish."

"It's what I wish, but only if you wish it too."

"It is settled then."

At the door, he gently kissed my hand.

"I am so happy that you are here, in Joplin," he whispered.

My head was beginning to spin. My stomach was full of butterflies. I so wished I didn't have to walk through that door without him. I slowly opened the door and went inside. As the door closed, I leaned against it not wanting to move away. Was this for real? I thought I would explode. Should I run after him and make sure he's going to come back? Don't be a silly goose—he'll be back.

I must have been noisy enough climbing the stairs to wake Mama.

"Oh, you're finally home," she said, coming out of her room in her robe and slippers. "How was the Christmas party?"

"It was wonderful," I said.

"What happened to you? Who did you meet?" I must have been glowing, and Mama had a way of noticing that about me.

"I'm not sure how to tell you this, and I do not want you to be mad because he is going to church with me in the morning and coming here for dinner after church."

"He?"

"Yes, he was there tonight. He came back here early just to see me... to find me."

"Who is he?"

"The Englishman...the actor, Cliff Hastings."

Mama frowned. "Your pa's not going to like this..." She was shaking her head.

"It's okay, Mama. It will be okay, and you need to help me make Papa understand. Cliff has genuine feelings for me and he wants to spend some time with me before he starts the winter season. I won't have much time with him, so Papa needs to...he needs to accept what is...not what he wants for me. I have feelings for Cliff...I always have."

She gave me that hopeless look. "It's late. I will talk to him, hopefully, well before the *actor* shows up to take you to church."

I fell asleep after about an hour of trying to figure out why Cliff had really come back to Joplin before his season started. He didn't seem like a man with bad intentions like Miss Claredon warned me about. I knew he was well thought of amongst the members of his company as being a kind and honorable man. But he was a charmer, Miss Claredon said, when she reminded me that his female fans were Cliff's priority and that any hope of being more than a friend was hopeless. But a little voice that sounded like Olive reminded me not to come across as some young, pathetic "Joplin git" without a brain in her head. I was an older and better educated lady. I should expect to be treated like a lady, and if he had other ideas, well, I wasn't interested. Tonight was about champagne, and singing and fun. Just wait and see how he is in the morning. I just hoped he'd show up tomorrow.

23

The greatest happiness of life is the conviction that we are loved~
loved for ourselves, or rather loved in spite of ourselves.
~**Victor Hugo (1802-1885)**

I was dressed and ready for church by nine. My hair was pinned up under a big forest green velvet bonnet that matched my forest green velvet dress trimmed in white lace with small red roses. I had a full-length green velvet coat to match, just a little something I had purchased in Kansas City. I pinched my cheeks to make them rosy and colored my lips a deep red, so I was ready to see him. I just hoped that he wanted to see me.

Then I remembered I had to explain all of this to Papa, and there was no way Papa was going to make this day easy on me. Papa was Irish through and through, and he did not favor the English, much less "traveling actors." He had made it clear to me several times that he did not want his only child running off with one. It was doubtful he would tolerate having Cliff over for Christmas dinner.

Papa came out to the front room dressed in his Sunday "goin to church" suit. I was mulling over how I was going to tell him about Cliff.

"So the Englishman showed up here last night?"

"Yes."

"Just out of the blue?"

"Yes."

"And he's taking you to church today?"

"Yes."

"You asked him over for dinner?"

"Yes."

"Good...I think he likes brandy. I'll stop by the saloon and get some."

"That would be real nice, Papa."

"And some cigars."

"Okay, Papa."

"How long do you reckon he is here for?"

"He is here for the winter season at the Club."

"Okay," Papa said as he left the room. I was surprised, more like shocked that he had nothing more to say on the subject of the Englishman.

Mama and Papa left for church a little early because she had some food to deliver for the Christmas reception after the service. At about nine thirty, there was a knock at the door.

"You're a sight for sore eyes," Cliff said when I opened the door.

I looked at him, not knowing what to say. "Hello," I managed to squeak.

He looked at me with his head cocked sideways. "You didn't believe that I would come?" he asked as he took my hand and kissed it.

"I hoped you would be here, but I wasn't even sure if you were real."

"You keep saying that...what do I have to do to convince you that I am real?" he asked. "Here pinch me, it will hurt and...I will cry out." He offered me his arm as if he was really expecting me to pinch him. "I am not only real, but I am thrilled to be here and to be able to go to Christmas church with the most beautiful and talented piano player in the world on my arm."

He made me laugh. "Well, hopefully no one will recognize you at church, or it will not be such a thrilling experience for either one of us I fear. I can just hear all the ladies talking about you, 'Who is that man with Marie?'"

"Marie?" He looked at me with an arched brow.

"Yes, I am Marie now. That is my middle name... I like it better, for now."

He smiled. "I'm glad you told me that...it would not have looked too good on my part if I didn't even know your name. How do you plan to introduce me?"

"I don't know. Do you have a suggestion?"

"Yes, actually I do. My God-given name is Clifford Priest. Introduce me as Clifford Priest."

"Clifford Priest…okay…that might work. I fear the name *Clifford* is a dead giveaway though. We don't have too many *Cliffords* around these parts with your English accent. Just don't open your mouth and start singing one of your Vaudeville specialties." I joked. "By the way, Mr. Priest, you look very debonair. I will tell everyone that you are a good friend of mine from Kansas City." Could I tell a lie with a straight face?

"What do I do for a living?"

"That depends. What part do you want to play today?"

"Anything but an actor."

"I'll tell them that you run your own business. But I cannot lie to them—they will all be seeing you at the Club in a few weeks."

"You can tell them whatever you want…you found me in the street gutter…I don't care. Just don't tell them who I am, as in don't say my stage name." His eyes were teasing me, but I could tell underneath he was being serious. He pulled me closer, gave me a sweet kiss, and then opened the door. When we reached his car, he opened the car door and helped me into my seat. He was a gentleman. I could tell the ladies at the church that he was certainly a gentleman.

"I have something for you," he said as he handed me a small gift.

"Oh, I haven't had the time to get you something for Christmas. You gave me no warning."

"The only thing I want from you right now is your time. I truly have everything I want right here, right now."

I unwrapped the box. Inside was a small diamond pendant the shape of a piano. It was on a gold chain. It was the most beautiful piece of jewelry I had ever seen and so perfect for me.

"It's beautiful…and so perfect for me. I'll wear it always and think of you."

"Let me put it on you." He clasped the chain around my neck. It fit perfectly with my dress.

"I love it!" I said as I put my hand over the pendant.

"It is given with love," he said and touched my cheek. He was certainly charming me.

We were one of the last people to arrive at the church. Cliff planned it that way so he could sit in the back corner. Hopefully, not many people would notice us. It would not be an enjoyable experience for me or for him if he was recognized.

After the service, we went with the others to the church basement for the Christmas reception. Several of the ladies of the church approached us and asked to meet him, and I rightfully introduced him as Clifford Priest from Kansas City. Mrs. Papals said that Mr. Priest looked familiar to her, and she wondered if he had been here before. He acknowledged that he had been to Joplin before and that it was likely that they had seen each other before. Even when the ladies left our side, I could tell they were all talking about the handsome young Englishman with Marie Lawton.

Mama just smiled when they asked her about him. She knew better than to say he was an actor. Papa was outside smoking his pipe and talking to the men about baseball.

"Are you ready to go?" I said.

"Only if you are," he replied.

"I'm ready."

As we walked to the car, I heard him say, "Well, that went well...I had forgotten how nice it was to be anonymous...just another bloke in the crowd. It is great fun to watch people and how they behave in regular life with one another."

"I'm glad such simple things amuse you. There's a park over there. Do you want to walk?" I asked.

"Sure, I could use the fresh air."

"Do you want to smoke?"

"No, I'm trying to quit the nasty habit, but I haven't quite given up my pipe."

He reached for my hand.

"May I hold your hand?" he said with a smile.

"I'd love for you to hold my hand. Maybe I'll actually learn something about you by holding your hand. I feel like there is so much about you I don't know."

"There is a lot you do not know about me, a boat load of information that's not important. What's important is what is right here," he padded his heart with his hand, "and I think you know about that." Cliff was still being a charmer.

"Where is your family?"

"Bristol, England."

"When did you come here?"

"In 1905. I was eighteen."

"Have you ever been married?"

"Never."

"Have you ever wanted to be married?"

"Sometimes, but in this life the opportunity does not arise all that often."

"What do you mean? You have so many women gushing over you all the time. You could have your pick."

"That's not how it works for me. Life on the road is actually pretty lonely. I have been alone a long time now, it seems."

I must have looked skeptical.

"Yes, there have been a lot of effusive women, but no one that is my soul mate or that I want to be bonded to for life. That's what marriage is for me. I watch Vic and Eunice. It has not been an easy go for them. Our life is not easy on a marriage, especially when the unwritten rules are that you have to keep that part of your life so separate from the stage world."

"Yes, Miss Claredon explained that to me."

"Oh, she did?"

"Yes, she warned me to stay away from you."

He rolled his eyes, ran his hand through his hair, and smiled. "Now that does not surprise me. I suspect that you weren't the first person she had that conversation with." He shook his head. "You know, I would gladly bring you into my world when you are ready for it. But you have to be strong and confident, and you have to know when people are feeding you a line of bull. And above all, you would have to know that you can trust me above all else. The world that I live in is full of illusion. It is all about illusion. You would need to know in your heart what is real. Those are my terms."

"I'm not sure I would be ready for your world."

"I doubt that you are, but if you ever think you're willing to give it a go, tell me. I would take you with me in a minute."

"You mean take me with you, on your terms?"

"Yes, you could play your piano in so many wonderful places."

"I would be another one of your performers?"

"No, you wouldn't." He was struggling again for words. "You could be whatever you wanted. And, of course you could, if you chose, be a performer. But you have to know that this life that I lead, that you would lead, all this traveling, disruption, and pretense is not going to last forever. There will come a time, probably in the not too distant future, when the expertise being developed in the film industry will change everything. Moving pictures, especially the talkies, will have a huge impact on our business once they develop the equipment. We're already seeing theaters converting over to picture houses. We all know in this business that we have a limited period of time before movies take over most of the theaters out here."

"Then what do you plan to do? Miss Claredon said you would never marry."

"She told you that?" He ran his hand through his hair again. "That's a bunch of bull...I can marry as long as I am not public with the marriage. I'm not even sure what that means."

"What would you do if live theater performances come to an end?"

"I would hope that there will always be live theater—it just will not be as prevalent and profitable as it is now. There were some forty thousand people working in live theater when I first came to America and over three hundred touring productions each year. More and more theaters are converting over to moving pictures each year. I fear the touring company that I have come to know is a dying breed."

"So you think this is all going to end?"

"Not completely, but eventually my time as a traveling stage actor will end, and I'll have to find some other way to earn my keep. Perhaps I'll settle down in one place with my wife and raise a family. I do know one thing. I want you with me."

Now was not a good time to ask him whether he would go to Hollywood and make moving pictures. It sounded as if he would be willing to take me with him wherever he was going and that he might be willing to help me become a performer, maybe an actress. Was he proposing marriage to me or just suggesting I become his companion? Where was this conversation going? Did I dare explain how I felt? He was being so sweet. I had to say something to him.

"Cliff, I do have feelings for you, but I have never allowed myself to acknowledge, much less share, those feelings. I was told you were off limits...and that even a friendship with you was forbidden. So I've locked all those feelings away, and now you tell me I can unlock the door, that you want me to unlock the door. I need some time to think about this."

"I know that you need time...I really do. It is difficult for me to be complacent about our time together. Unfortunately, we will have so very little time together once the season gets started...But please, don't think that I expect anything from you, other than your honesty. I certainly do not want to rush you into a decision that you might regret."

In the middle of the park on a Christmas day in Joplin, Missouri, this tall, handsome actor took me in his arms and kissed me like no one ever had. During that moment, I thought that I already knew what my decision would have to be.

When we arrived back home, Mama and Aunt Maggie were busy getting Christmas dinner ready. Mama was preparing a delicious roast according to her mother's special recipe. I joined them in the kitchen to help. At least I knew how to properly set a table and fold the napkins. Cliff went in the living room and sat with Papa and Uncle Sam. I noticed Cliff walk over to my piano and look closely at the photographs of me as a child on the top of my piano. I just knew he was looking to find that little girl by the creek. Papa gave him a glass of brandy, and every once in a while I heard them laugh out loud. They must have been swapping stories or talking about baseball because Papa loved his baseball.

24

Disappointment is the nurse of wisdom.
~ **BAYLE ROCHE (1736–1807)**

Cliff graciously complemented Mama and Aunt Maggie on their most delicious Christmas dinner. After dinner, I asked Cliff if he would walk with me to look at all the decorations. It would give me more time with him alone because we had a lot to talk about.

"Thank you for inviting me to dinner. It has been a long time since I had Christmas dinner at someone's home."

"Christmas dinner is our family tradition. What do you usually do?" Mama asked.

"Honestly, I do not know...nothing special...I am usually on the road. Sometimes we do a special Christmas show at a local hospital, just singing carols for the patients, mainly children, who cannot be at home on Christmas, and that has always been a humbling experience."

"How thoughtful of you," I said as I touched his arm.

"I'm just thankful to be the one singing."

The town was lit up with Christmas lights and other decorations. There weren't many people out and about. The trolleys weren't even working. It was probably the only day of the year that the trolleys were shut down.

We walked past the front of the Criterion. Papa had a few decorations in the window, but otherwise it was dark and locked up. Cliff stopped to peer in the saloon window.

I noticed a lady standing on the street. She glanced my way and quickly turned her head. She looked familiar, so I walked over to her.

"Cora? Is that you?" I knew it had to be her. She was in a red dress with a black overcoat and a big red hat. She had a black fur muff around her hands. "Cora, it's me, Della...Adella Lawton." I reached out to her and she took my hand.

"Della," she said my name as she looked nervously over my shoulder at Cliff.

"How are you? I thought you had moved out of town?"

"Well, I'm livin' right here...been here a while," she said.

A heavyset man stepped out of a side door and grabbed her arm. I did not recognize him as being from Joplin, at least not from my neighborhood.

"Come on now," he commanded to Cora.

"Just a minute, Ben...Can I have a minute? This is an old friend of mine, and I haven't seen her in such a long time," Cora said.

"I ain't got all day," he said and he grabbed at her again.

I heard a man's voice behind me say, "Let the ladies have a minute." It was Cliff. The man with Cora stiffened and glared at Cliff.

Cora handed me a slip of paper with a room number on it. "Della, come see me next week, Monday, before noon, if you can. I work at a saloon, and I stay upstairs." She walked away with the man dragging her by the arm down the street, as I stood there afraid to move. I could hear his voice scolding her as they walked away but could not make out what he was saying.

"I have to go see her," I mumbled to myself as it dawned on me what had become of my childhood friend, Cora.

"The hell you will," Cliff mumbled back as he gently took my arm and began walking with me in the other direction.

Tears started to fall on my cheeks. I covered my mouth with my hand to try to hold them back.

"That was my friend, Cliff...my friend. What have they done? Little, innocent Cora. They made her a..." I couldn't say it. "That man, he was so vile. Cora, she was such a beautiful child."

He took me to a bench and sat me down as the tears poured out of me. "I didn't know...I didn't know." I covered my eyes with my hands. All I could think of was all the charity work I had done with the church, all of the baskets of food and clothes that we delivered to the poor, and Cora was there all along, and I didn't help her. What kind of a creature was her mother to let that happen to her daughter?

"Della, listen to me," Cliff said, handing me a handkerchief. "I'm not going to let you go see her alone. It's not safe. I will accompany you to see her on Monday, if you wish, and then you must find the strength to walk away. Cora has made a choice, and if she wanted another way of life, she could have come to you. This is not your fault, love."

Cliff put his arm around me and held me close while I processed the situation that I found my childhood friend in. I finally looked at him. "I'm sorry for being so upset. It just took me by surprise. I was not expecting to see her this way. I don't know what I was expecting. She could have done so much more with her life."

"That's the story with all of those ladies who live above saloons. Unfortunately there are a lot of them out here in these mining towns. They all could have done better, but they didn't, and there is nothing you or I can do to change that fact."

"I don't want to see her like this." I was angry.

"Do you still want to go see her on Monday?"

"Yes."

"Are you going to be able to walk away when your visit is done?"

"Yes," I said with a little less confidence.

Cliff smiled. "That's my girl. Now let us think about something more cheerful as we walk back to your place."

"Is your hotel close by?" I wanted to know where he lived and to see how he lived.

"It is."

"Can we go there?" It was a completely innocent request on my part.

"No." He was being serious.

"Why not?"

"Right now, it would not be a proper thing for me to do...to take you to my hotel."

"Not proper..." That was all I could say. How ironic. I couldn't get the man who I adored to show me his room, while my friend was being dragged down the street by a vile creature of a man that she hated.

"You Englishmen are quite proper, aren't you?" I finally said. "Just to set the record straight, I was not suggesting that we go there for any reason other than for you to show me where you live."

"Then you can consider the record set straight...Now, tell me your favorite childhood memory," he said with a jovial smile on his face, swiftly changing the subject.

By the time we reached my home, we were laughing and joking. After all of that business with Cora, he had gotten me back into the Christmas spirit. By nightfall, I could tell he had to leave but I did not want Cliff to go. He was the first to speak about it.

"Marie, I don't want to leave you, but I am afraid that I must. Vic and Eunice arrived tonight, and I really need to talk to Vic before they turn in. But I have an idea. I will pick you up tomorrow morning—we can go to church if you like. It would probably be a good idea for you to show up in time for your choir performance." He laughed to himself. "Then we'll have lunch. Anywhere you want to go, in Joplin, of course. Then, if you want, we'll go visit Vic and Eunice—that way you can see where I'm going to live and it will be a proper, respectable visit. What do you think?"

I suddenly remembered the note from Jenkins. "Cliff...I really have to talk to you about this....you and I...I don't know how to put this so it sounds right..."

"Just put it out there. I'm a big boy." He looked at me like he thought I was going to banish him from my life. "Tell me, please, what is it?"

"Well you know how you are not allowed to publicly have a relationship with a woman? It applies to me as well. I cannot see you, publicly. I really cannot see you at all. I will lose my job."

"Who says so?"

"Jenkins. He gave me a list of rules. I am not allowed to fraternize with performers." I could barely pronounce the word *fraternize* right.

He belted out a laugh, "Oh, is that what they call what we are doing, fraternizing?" He was not taking me seriously.

"I fear between Jenkins and your theater women, this isn't going to work," I tested him.

"Listen." He touched my face. "You let me take care of everything. You're very important to me, and I am not going to hide that from the whole world. We can be discreet to the theater public, but I will not hide you from my world, and I will not accept that you cannot be in my life." He gently lifted my chin and kissed me, long and deep and wonderful. "I will explain to Jenkins, and we will make this work," he whispered. "I promise you that. The theater women…well…they can just go to hell."

25

*First, you have to get used to sharing the man you love with
the public and used to the fact that they are...we are...always
pretending to be someone who we are not and saying words we do
not mean to people who are also pretending. There is no room here
for a jealous lover—*

~EUNICE VICKERY

The Sunday after Christmas came soon enough. I was beginning to get worried about Cliff being recognized as the actor Clifford Hastings at church. If he was recognized, they would likely annoy him, if not stampede him.

He showed up promptly at nine thirty, and I was ready for him.

"Cliff? I have an idea. In fact, I think it's a pretty good idea, but I don't want you to take it the wrong way."

"Yes, love?" he said softly as he took my hand. I think it was an English thing to call everyone dear to them "love."

"Someone in the church is going to figure out who you are...and it will be awkward if they do. So why don't we sit far in the back, I will join the choir when needed, and then we will quietly leave."

"You mean miss the church reception?"

"Yes, I mean miss the church reception. The ladies gossip there, and I know one of them is bound to recognize you."

"Good idea, Marie." He was quiet for a moment. "I have something to tell you. I went to see Jenkins this morning to get the key to the theater. Let's just say that Jenkins and I had a talk."

"That was fast."

"It was important," he said as he took my hand. "I think he will be okay with you and I being together if we remain discreet, at least around the theater. But I have to tell you...he was harder on me than your father."

"Really? Jenkins gave you a hard time."

"He questioned me about my intentions and whether they were honorable toward you...But I think after talking to me that old Jenkins could tell that I had fallen."

"What's that mean?"

"Oh something like I'm 'head over heels' for you," he said as he took me in his arms and started to slow dance with me.

"You act like you're going to break into a song any minute."

"And what if I did? Would you join me?" he challenged.

"Not here on my way to church," I replied, "but I'll sing with you sometime, Clifford Hastings, in the right place, at the right moment."

After church, we went to lunch at the *Cup n' Saucer* in downtown Joplin. I was not real hungry, so I ordered a small cup of chicken soup, while Cliff had tea and a sandwich.

"Vic and Eunice are renting a house, and I have moved in with them. It has five bedrooms, so I think there will be a few more of the troupe moving in as well." Cliff said.

"That will be much better for you than a hotel." I hated to think of him living in a hotel. It would be so cold and lonesome.

"I really don't mind hotels. I'm so used to living on the road, but I do like it when a group of us can get into a real house. There is so much more privacy."

"So are you going to take me there?"

"Yes, I will. Vic and Eunice are hoping to see you today."

The house was a large Queen-Anne style home on Byers Street that belonged to a Joplin family who was away that winter. They were loyal patrons of the Club Theater, so they allowed certain performers to use the house in their absence. The house was made of stone and had beautiful curved bay windows in the front, a cupola, and a huge lawn with a garden area that would be lush with flowers in the spring.

When we arrived, both Eunice and Vic met us at the front door, which displayed a large Christmas wreath made of pine and red ribbons.

"Miss Lawton," they both chimed in together as they hugged me.

"Oh, please, you must call me Marie," I said as I made my way through the front door. Cliff stayed behind me a few steps.

The home was furnished beautifully. It had hardwood floors with Persian rugs, a large staircase in the front going upstairs that was trimmed in holiday garland, a library, and best of all, a sitting room with a baby grand piano. There was a kitchen and a formal dining room in the back of the house and a room to the side with a large desk that was an office. Papers and drawings were scattered all over the desk, and it looked like someone, probably Vic, had been working in that room.

"Marie, would you care for some tea?" Eunice offered.

"I would love some tea," I said as I removed my coat into Cliff's waiting hands.

"Come on back. I'll show you my kitchen. It's not often that I get to have my own kitchen." Eunice chuckled as she led me to the back of the house.

"Marie, I'm going to borrow Cliff for a while. We have some matters to discuss. We'll just be in the office," Vic called out.

"Don't worry if we're not here when you finish," Eunice joked as she continued walking me back to her kitchen.

I heard Cliff say, "What's going on?" as he walked into the office. "I can see you made yourself plenty at home in here already." The door to the office closed.

The kitchen was large and all white with small china blue tiles interspersed with larger white tiles. There was a large kitchen island in the middle and a table and chairs toward the back of the kitchen in an alcove with large windows that overlooked another garden. This little spot would be beautiful in the spring when the flowers bloomed.

Eunice put the teapot on the stove and set the table in the rear with teacups, cream, and sugar.

"Vic is having some real issues with the winter season we are about to start, and I know he wants Cliff's input. Cliff is real good at finding solutions. I don't know what Vic would do without him." She sat down at the table and motioned me to sit with her as she poured us both a steaming cup of hot tea.

"You have grown into a beautiful young lady, Marie. Last time I saw you…you were a child. I understand that you spent some time in Kansas City in school. Cliff said your mother wanted you home because of the war overseas."

"Yes, although I was not quite ready to come back to Joplin. I really enjoyed my time in Kansas City. I figure I'll stay around here for a while yet, and then I'll go back and finish my schooling. I was a piano teacher for school children in Kansas City."

"Oh, it's too bad Abigail, my daughter, is not with us. I would hire you to teach her piano. But she's with her grandparents in St. Louis so she can go to school. We spent Christmas Eve with her in St. Louis. Came by train yesterday so we could get started. Lots of work to do."

"How old is she now?" I inquired.

"Abby's eleven."

"That is a good age to learn music. My students in Kansas City were all about eleven or twelve years old." We both were silent for a few minutes.

"You know, Marie, I was really hoping that we could be alone to talk. And here we are, and I'm all tongue-tied. I want you to know that I have known Cliff a long time. He is a good man, not your typical egotistical, leading male actor." She paused. "He has been around a lot of women… women that have literally thrown themselves at him. He gets tons of letters in every place we play. People follow him, photograph him, and hound him for his autograph. People steal things from him, just to have a souvenir. I guess what I'm trying to tell you is that he is the real thing and he has always behaved honorably as far as I am concerned."

"I appreciate you telling me this…but I'm just not sure where I fit into all of this."

"I have never seen him as happy as he is right now, with you, here. I know he had special feelings for you when we were here before. I think he thought you were a musical genius or something like that, because you could play almost anything anyone put in front of you. He respected you more than anyone, and he admired your knowledge and the intensity you felt toward your music. But you were so young. Cliff, if he is anything, he is an honorable man first. He's British after all, raised in a very proper family… But I think it was very difficult for him to ignore his feelings for you back then. He is twenty-eight years old now, and you must be around twenty-three?"

"No, I am only eighteen."

Eunice put her hand to her mouth as if to stop herself from saying something she shouldn't. "Oh," she said.

That was the first time I had heard any mention of Cliff's family. There was silence again.

"You know when it all came out? It all came out when he realized that you were that little girl that he and Vic rescued down by the creek. I think your father told him the night before we left town. He could not believe that she was you. That man could not stop talking about you. Then I think it all fell in place for him, like this thing between you two was meant to be. Vic and I used to think maybe performing in all of these melodramas had gone to his head. But I do not think for a moment that he ever stopped thinking about you and counting the days when he would be back here with you, in Joplin."

"But I had no idea...he didn't even write to me."

"I'm sure he had his reasons for that, and I have no doubt that they are honorable."

"What does he expect of me...do you know?"

"I have only an idea of what he expects of you, but I'll tell you what I expect. I want you to be truthful with him. Do not lead him into thinking that you feel the same way about him if you do not. He is too good a person, and he is so very important to our company as a performer. I do not want to see him get shattered by the first woman I think he has ever truly loved."

"I do have feelings for him, and I did back then. But it seemed all so one-sided and in my head, like a teenage fling. I had no idea what he thought of me. This is all so new to me, but I don't want to do anything that would hurt him. I just have to figure out my life and how he fits into it, I guess."

"You're very right. You do need to think long and hard about this before you jump," she said. "I will not kid you that this life that Vic and I lead is not easy. It has gotten easier for me after ten years, but it is never without its setbacks. First, you have to get used to sharing the man you love with the public and used to the fact that they are...we are...always pretending to be someone who we are not and saying words we do not mean to people who are also pretending. There is no room here for a jealous lover—I'll tell you that…especially with Cliff. He invariably will play the male lead who is some other woman's lover, usually played by a beautiful actress, who would jump at the chance to play with her leading man off the stage. Can you live with that? Then, if you marry him, you cannot publicly take his name. You will always be known, as long as you are in stock, as Miss Marie Lawton. Can you live with that? Then there are the receptions with his adoring fans. You are not a part of that with him, and his fans have no idea who you are nor do they care. Can you live with that? Then, you have to realize to a certain extent his anonymity is gone. It becomes very difficult to go anywhere and lead a normal life, especially when we have been playing an extended season in one location. The fans get to know him. They follow him, flock to him in public, write him letters and cards, throw themselves at his feet, or sometimes even threaten him, and you are expected to smile and enjoy it all, to a point. Can you handle that? In addition, the work that they do is exhausting. They no sooner learn the lines and blocking for one show, and they're starting another show. Sure, they have an established repertory of shows, but that is constantly changing and being updated. They are always looking for ways to do something different, or funnier, or better. The stage is a jealous lover. It demands all of their time and all of their attention, most of the time." She looked at me, and I could not speak.

"If you can honestly say, yes, 'I can handle all of those things, Eunice,' then you have to think about what it's like to be on the road constantly and living out of a suitcase or a trunk. You never have your own home, and the longest you might be in one place is six months. You do not own many things because you have to travel light. Restaurant food becomes very mundane after a while. You have to like to travel, to see new places, and meet new people. You have to be prepared to meet and greet people who you despise but who might have a huge influence over your husband's success or failure. I'll tell you, it has been an exciting life…I'm never bored. Oh, I almost forgot, then there are the injuries."

"Injuries?"

"Injuries…these guys play hard on the stage, and they more often than not, get hurt…sometimes real hurt." She got up and left the room for a minute. When she came back in, she was reading out loud from a newspaper clipping in an album.

"*Cliff Hastings, who is playing leads with the Garside Stock Company, which is playing an indefinite engagement at the Arcade Theatre, in Paducah, Kentucky, recently gave his audience a touch of realism when his company was playing 'In the Heart of Alaska.' In one scene there is a roughhouse and Mr. Hastings accidentally slipped and fell and sustained a scalp wound and body bruises. He finished the play but when he walked from the stage he fell in a faint. His injuries did not keep him from the following performances however."*

She looked up at me with her hands waving in the air. "Marie, he had a bleeding concussion, a huge gash in his head, and he passed the hell out, and he still finished the show."

I shook my head in disbelief.

"And you may as well kiss any privacy you ever had good-bye," she added. "Everything that happens to him, if the press gets wind of it, it gets reported in the paper. Look at this article, some hotel clerk stole Cliff's shoes, and he turned him in. It got reported. Now tell me, who really cares about Cliff's shoes?" Eunice read the article out loud to me.

"When Cliff Hastings, an actor with the Garside Stock Company saw a pair of his patent leather shoes walking around the premises on the feet of Jim Couch, colored, the hired boy at his boarding house, Seventh and Jefferson Streets, he decided that Couch was apt to be wearing more of his wardrobe before long and he went after the police. Patrolmen Hugh Garrett and Ellis Stewart, traffic men, were ushered to the Boarding House where Couch was arrested and taken before Police Judge Cross just as court had adjourned. Justice was speedy and in less than five minutes, Couch was en route to Sixth and Clark Streets in a rubber tired vehicle known as the police ambulance and accepted an invitation to inspect the interior of the County Jail. Couch contended that he bought the "kicks" off a white boy without a name near Fourth and Jefferson Streets about two weeks ago in the midst of a snowfall. Police Judge Cross sized up the shoe merchant as being just about as big as Couch, of the same color and of the same shape and he held him over to the grand jury on $100 bail for petit larceny."

"Now, tell me, why did this article even get into the paper to begin with? Cliff was not happy about this one."

My head was starting to swim. What was she trying to tell me? "This is a lot to think about…" That was all I could say to her.

"Tell me one thing…Do you love him?" Eunice asked.

I had not said those words to Cliff, so it took me a minute to answer her.

"He has not heard those words from me yet."

"That is not what I asked. Do. You. Love. Him?"

"Yes…at least, I think so, but I am not ready to let him know that."

"Why not?" She was not going to let me off the hook easy.

"Well, there are a lot of reasons, but mainly...I just saw him again after a year and a half on Friday night. It is now Sunday afternoon. I need more time. I am eighteen years old. I don't know what love is. I've never had a serious relationship. But ever since he has been here, I have done nothing but think of him. I want to be with him every moment. I want to spend as much time as I can with him, and I want to work with him and help him in any way I can. I never want him to leave my side at night, and I lay awake thinking about being with him. I want to find ways to make him happy. I love his smile. I love that he is so protective of me and so very thoughtful. I cannot imagine there ever being another man in my life... Does this sound like love to you?"

"It sounds like you've got it pretty bad, honey." Eunice smiled. I think she was relieved to know that this thing between Cliff and I was not one-sided after all.

26

I have learned that to be with those I like is enough.
~WALT WHITMAN (1819-1892)

C liff walked into the kitchen. He had taken his coat off, and his sleeves were rolled up to his elbow. He had a pencil tucked in behind his ear like he always had during rehearsals. As he walked up to my chair, he reached out to put his hands on my shoulders.

"Hey, Eunice, are you keeping Marie entertained? Your husband has been in there messing around with my sets. It looks like I'm going to have to make a trip to the lumberyard this week. Soon."

"Well, we've been having a nice talk...I've actually been doing all the talking," Eunice offered.

"Now that worries me. Don't listen to a thing she says, Marie. She's a dangerous lady, that one," Cliff said as he sat down at the table next to me.

Eunice was nothing like Elise, who thankfully was not in this company.

"Who you calling a dangerous lady?" Vic walked in the kitchen. "Eunice ain't no lady."

She got up and socked Vic in the arm. "You be good or I won't cook you any supper, you worm," she teased.

"Promise?" Vic quipped back to her. I could tell through all this teasing around that they were still very much in love. It was my turn for questions, and I had a lot of them.

"Now that you are all here, will one of you please tell me about your winter season in Joplin?" I asked.

"Can't do that," Cliff quipped. "Vic has no idea what we are doing, do you, Vic?"

"Actually, Cliff can't do that because he doesn't have a clue what we are doing."

Cliff arched his brow, put his hand on his chin, and looked at Vic intently.

"I, on the other hand, can answer your question with upmost knowledge and sincerity because I have been anxiously studying this particular subject for days on end," Vic said almost like he was playing some character in a play.

"Please," Cliff said sarcastically.

"Well?" I said to Vic.

"Well?" Cliff chimed in looking at Vic.

Vic looked at me, took a deep breath, and said, "We're going to start running plays, one a week, after New Years. We probably will have three to four shows a week depending upon attendance. Most likely, Thursday through Saturday, with two shows on Saturday. I am not sure yet whether we will do a Monday or Tuesday show. We have most of the shows figured out, but we have a few minor details to work on, Cliff." He looked over at Cliff, who just smiled back. "The winter season here should take us through March and possibly into the first two weeks of April. I am not yet sure. Then we are off for the spring and summer to Des Moines, Iowa, and to St. Joseph, Missouri, where we have solid bookings through September." He stopped to take a breath. "I expect we will spend most of the spring-summer season in St. Joseph. Have you ever been there?"

"It's where Jesse James was killed," Eunice said.

"Overall, a dandy place to be," Cliff added.

"Wow, you sure rattled off all of that information fast." I looked at Vic in amazement.

"I am pretty amazing," Vic said proudly.

"Yes, an amazing fool you are," Eunice quipped.

"Please…You may think you are on top now, old chap, but tomorrow you could be managing a Nickelodeon," Cliff said.

"See what I have to live with?" Vic said as he looked over at me and pointed to the two of them.

"I have one more question," I said.

"Only one?" Cliff said.

"Shoot," Vic said.

"Are you going to need me for specialties?" I asked.

"Hell yes, we are," Cliff interrupted.

"Listen to Mr. Vaudeville over here," Vic said mockingly. They all knew Cliff loved his Vaudeville.

"That's what keeps them coming back, Mr. Hollywood," Cliff replied.

"Ooh…ouch that one hurt," Vic replied, grasping his chest as if he'd been punched. Eunice grimaced. I guess everyone was well aware of Cliff's contempt for Hollywood and moving pictures. To Cliff, Hollywood was a famished predator of the traveling theater troupes.

"Do you want to know the real fun thing about this season?" Cliff said to me.

"Yes, sure," I said hesitantly, not knowing what was going to come out of his mouth next, fact or fiction.

"The Macks, as we refer to them, are our booking agents and managers. They are on holiday. So Mr. Hollywood over here is going to produce and direct the first four plays."

I looked at Vic. "Really?"

He nodded. He was quite proud. "And Mr. Vaudeville over here has the lead in all of them," Vic retorted.

I looked at Cliff. "What plays are you doing?"

"Well, first we are doing *Thorns and Orange Blossoms,* which is an adaptation of Bertha M. Clay's celebrated novel of English life. I get to play Lord Randolph Ryvers, who while traveling in Spain on business trip, becomes involved with a singer. It's too bad she's not a piano player," he added. "My friend convinces me to forget the singer and return to New Orleans, where my girlfriend awaits. The Spanish singer follows me to New Orleans. I manage to secretly elope with my girlfriend. We plan a wedding to be held at my girlfriend's, now wife's, home. When I find out that my Spanish singer plans to disrupt the wedding, I plead with her. She has a gun and ends up getting shot and having me arrested for it. Then, this Spanish tart discovers that I am a married man and that my wife has a baby, so she comes clean and helps to get me released so I can live happily ever after with my family. Sound like a fun show?"

I smiled at him. I really did love listening to him speak with that wonderful accent.

He continued. "Then we are doing William Faversham's great international success, *'The Squaw Man'*. It's a comedy-drama written by Edwin Milton Royale. I think it was first done around 1907 in New York. I play John Roseleigh and Harry gets to play the attorney. Harry likes playing the bad guys. Did I mention that both of these plays have four acts?"

"What about Eunice?" I questioned.

"Oh, she'll be with Harry getting him dressed back stage." Cliff quipped, while everyone laughed.

"Then we are going to do *'Our Boys in Blue'* because Mr. Vaudeville is feeling a bit patriotic these days." Vic chimed in.

"You know, it's pretty bad when us red coats support America more than you grey coats," Cliff said.

Vic sneered.

"But I hate to tell you this Marie, in this play he is cast as *'the Lover,'*" Vic added.

"That's it? No name, just 'the *Lover?*' I asked.

"And I'll be a damn good one at that." Cliff interrupted as everyone laughed again.

"And of course, we will be doing *Dora Thorne,* which is an adaptation of another one of Bertha Clay's novels," Vic offered. "And in that, Mr. Vaudeville plays Ronald Earle, and I am Stephen Thorne. Actually, this play was made into a silent film this past year with Lionel Barrymore in my part. I feel honored. It is a quite a romantic story."

"I figured as much," I said. "Cliff's fans love him best in the romantic roles."

"Just a typical melodrama about star-crossed lovers and meddling mothers. Something I've dearly missed having," Cliff said.

"A meddling mother or a star-crossed lover?" Vic quipped.

Cliff rolled his eyes. "Both," he said. "My favorite line, 'Dora Thorne is mine,'" Cliff said in full character.

"Who plays Dora Thorne?" I asked, not wanting to know the answer.

"None other than the beautiful, and charming, and talented, Bessie Jackson," Vic said.

"Well if you love Bessie so much, why don't you play Ronald Earle, Mr. Hollywood?" Cliff said. They were back at it again.

"I would if I had your dashing good looks, Mr. Vaudeville," Vic replied. "The rest of the season, Marie, is still under construction."

Eunice broke in changing the subject. "You know, Will Foster and Orrin Burke are going to be staying with us here. I think the ladies have a house of their own rented for the season," Eunice offered. "I think Jimmy McCoy will be here as well. I'm not sure who else."

"I really do not care who you bring over, as long as I have my own room," Cliff said.

"Plan on needing some privacy, Mr. Vaudeville?" Harry quipped. Cliff shot him a dirty look.

"If I was looking for privacy, Mr. Hollywood, I wouldn't be looking around here," Cliff replied.

"Let's cook up some supper," Eunice said.

After dinner, they all asked me to play the piano for them. Eunice made sure I had plenty of music. They all joined me at the piano and sang along. We had great fun together, and I could tell that these were really warm, loving, and wonderfully talented people. I could see myself on the road traveling with these people. They were a family.

When he took me home, Cliff asked me to sit in the car with him for a while.

"I hope this day did not overwhelm you, too much," he said as he put his arm around me.

"Not too much," I said. "You know, I really enjoyed my day. I learned things about you and your extended family that you could never have told me. Thank you."

"Are you ready to go see Cora tomorrow?" he asked as he took my hand.

"I've been trying not to think of it. I think I just want to make sure she is all right, by her definition, and then I can move on. Don't worry about me. I'll bring my gun for protection."

"Your gun? You carry a gun?" Cliff was startled. He looked me straight in the eye to make sure I was not kidding around.

"Yes, my father gave me a small derringer and taught me how to shoot it after that incident at the creek that you and I seem to avoid talking about. He never wanted me to be without protection. So I carry it with me in my purse or strapped to my leg under my skirt. I'm a pretty good shot."

"I didn't know I was courting Annie Oakley." He laughed.

I grinned back at him.

"And the only reason I don't bring up the creek is because it must have been a terrifying experience for you, so why should we dwell on it? I don't want to make you uncomfortable. But if you ever find that you want to talk about it, just tell me." He laughed quietly. "Oh....wait until Vic and Eunice hear about this. You would have been the last person on earth that I would have thought carried a gun, small or not. You're tougher than I thought."

"There's a lot of things that will surprise you about me, Mr. Vaudeville."

27

Be curious, not judgmental.
~WALT WHITMAN (1819-1892)

Monday came faster than I had expected. Cliff agreed to take me to see Cora, and then he had to go work with the rest of the crew on the set. He wanted me to take him to the Joplin lumber store. Eunice wanted to go shopping with us, so we promised to pick her up after the visit with Cora.

"Where are you taking Marie?" Eunice inquired.

"I think to the third floor of the House of Lords saloon downtown," Cliff replied.

"Isn't that a brothel?" Vic chimed in. "Hope she's not there for a job interview."

Cliff did not miss a beat. "Don't worry," he said. "She's taking her gun."

Then we both turned walked down the front stoop and left Vic and Eunice standing by the door with stunned looks on their faces. I did have my derringer strapped to my leg. I think Cliff was more worried that I was going to shoot him.

The House of Lords was one of the finest restaurants in Joplin, boasting of serving the most delicious steaks for miles around. When we got to the House of Lords, the place looked closed, but an adjoining door on the side of the building opened to a narrow staircase that went up one long flight of stairs and then another. When we got to the third floor, we went into a lobby or waiting area, and thankfully no one was around. I found Cora's room number on a door in the back of the building. Cliff and I had already agreed that he would wait for me in the lobby area. He did not sit down.

When I knocked on the door with the number 315, Cora opened it, smiled at me, quickly ushered me into the room, and closed the door. The room was small but well-kept, probably better than I expected.

"Della, I wasn't sure if you would really come," Cora said as she hugged me. I could smell the stale perfume and tobacco smoke in her hair.

"This is not exactly a place that I would have pictured myself coming to either," I slowly said, trying to find my next words. "Cora, I don't want to take up your time. I'm just here to make sure that you are all right."

"I'm all right, Della…I'm okay with this life. I dunno what else I would do, to tell you the truth."

"So you're telling me there is nothing I can do to get you the hell out of here?" I asked.

"Even if there was, I been doin' this so long now, to be honest, Della, I'm not sure I would go with you." She reached for my hand.

"Do they treat you okay?" I could see light bruises on her arm, and she had some scarring on her face.

"Mostly…better here than at some other places. They don't tolerate beatin's here by the men," she said. I cringed. There was a bottle next to her bed. She picked it up and drank some of it.

"What is that?" I asked.

"Absinthe…have you ever had any?"

I shook my head no.

"Do you want a taste?"

I really had to get out of here.

"No, thank you. I'm fine…really. Cora, how did this happen to you?"

"Oh, it was my Mama's idea, really. I remember very little about my first time."

"Your first time?"

"Oh, Della, all's I remember is being in a dark room, with only a dirty piece of cowhide on the dusty wooden floor. I must have been about thirteen. A small ray of light shone through a crack in the wall. I could see the dust in the air as it floated through the air on the ray of light. The door opened to the room, and a big man wearing breeches stepped up onto the floor of the room from the ground below. He closed the door behind him and put the wooden latch across the door. I couldn't see his face, Della, but I could smell the liquor as it rolled off his breath.

"'You're a bit of a youngin,' he said.

"'Yes, sir.'

"'Well git on down there on the floor,' he commanded.

"Then I moved to the cowhide and kneeled not knowing what this man wanted. He kneeled next to me on the cowhide."

I started to cry, and Cora handed me a cloth.

"The man asked me my name, and I told him. Then he done it."

"What did he do?"

"He made me have sex with him, Della."

"Oh, Cora. How can you do this?"

"It's no matter, anymore, Della."

There was nothing I could say. Even if she would come away with me, it would be real hard to get my society to accept her. Cora would always be known as what she was in this room. I wanted to leave.

"Cora, if you need anything, will you promise to come find me?"

"Yes."

We both knew I would probably not see her again.

"Well, I'd better get going...Cliff, he's waiting for me."

"Cliff? Is he your man?"

"Yes, a very good man."

"You take good care of him now, Della." She touched my arm.

"Thank you for seeing me, Cora. You take care now." I gave her a hug. She was so thin.

"Sure, you, too. See you around, now," she said as she let me go.

As I walked out of that room, Cliff met me, gave me a hug, and escorted me to the stairway. He could see in my eyes the discomfort that I was feeling. He could see that I had been crying.

As we quickly walked down the first flight of stairs, it dawned on me how the circumstances that people find themselves in can have such an impact on the rest of their lives. Sometimes people actually have a choice, and in Cora's case, it seemed she made her choice, right then and there as she looked me in the eyes. It may not have been the right choice for me, but Cora felt it was the right choice for her. I had given her an option, and she had turned me down. It took me a while to realize that the best gift that Cora gave me that day was her honesty. Without that, I would have probably wasted years trying to change the choices that she had made for her life.

"Cliff, what's absinthe?" I asked as we were walking back to the car.

"You should ask your father about that. What I know about it is very little. It's an alcoholic beverage of sorts, very high proof. For one, I think it's been banned. I also read somewhere that it is a dangerously addictive drink. It supposedly makes people crazy and causes men to murder their wives. Very peculiar beverage, but likely quite popular in these parts."

"Have you ever tasted it?"

"Heavens no, at least, not that I know of. I would have probably liked it too much. I do admit that I have been gin-rickied, but I have never become crazy or murdered anyone." He smiled. "Why do you ask?"

"Oh, Cora mentioned it." I did not want to tell him she had a bottle of it on her bed stand and she offered me a sip. And I did not want to discuss with him what had happened to Cora. I suspected he knew more about those things than I did.

"Absinthe is one spirit I would highly recommend you stay away from, my dear."

By Monday night, after a full day of running around Joplin and shopping with Cliff and Eunice, he brought me to my home. I had now missed two evening meals with Papa and Mama.

"Cliff, I have so much to do tomorrow. I am not sure when I can see you. I have a church choir practice and then a Girl's Charity Worker's meeting, and I have to find some time to practice for New Year's Eve."

"New Year's? Are you working?"

"Yes, I'm working a party New Year's Eve at the Club, and I do want to learn some new music." I figured that Cliff had a lot of work to do as well, and maybe a little break from me would give him some time to get things done.

"I realize that we both have work, but I do not want there to be a day this week that I don't spend some time with you, even if it's just an hour," he said. "Once show time starts, we will have so very little time, unless it's early morning or late at night. And I don't know how long I can bear to not see you. Oh…and by the way, I will be at that New Year's Eve party." He smiled a wicked smile.

"Well, you'll have to wear a mask," I replied. He laughed.

"You've got a point there." He walked me to the front porch, but before we got to the steps, he pulled me into the darkness on the side of the house and into his arms. His lips met mine and kissed me deeply until I thought I was going to faint. The world around us seemed to fade away.

"You know how bad I don't want to say good night to you right now?" he breathed in my ear as he pulled me close to him.

"So this must be how it feels to be in one of your melodramas?" I breathed back.

"Not hardly," he whispered. His forehead was touching mine. "This is very real for me, love."

I could not bring myself to say anything to him. I think he could tell it was getting harder for both of us to say good night. It wasn't like we could just run off and be alone together, was it? There were rules, and I was raised to obey those rules. I still had not told Cliff how I truly felt about him. This was only the fourth night we had really been together. Could I tell any man I loved him after four nights and have it mean anything? Then Olive's voice returned in my head, *"Is he just any man to you, Della?"*

28

I also predict, as you have heard me say before, that Hollywood will eventually be the death of the traveling troupe as we know it.

~CLIFFORD HASTINGS

Eunice was right; the newspaper was going to make it almost impossible for Cliff to go anywhere in town without being hounded by his adoring fans. The Tuesday morning newspaper had a lead article with his photograph. The headline read, "Stock Company Coming Here With Cliff Hastings In It." Once the town got a look at that article and his face, his anonymity would be gone.

By Tuesday afternoon, Mama said the ladies at the church were a talkin' away. They had figured out that Cliff Hastings was in fact the gentleman, *Clifford Priest,* who had accompanied me to church on two occasions. That was extraordinary news to them. Mama told me that some of the ladies were disturbed that I had not "properly introduced him" at church.

By the time I arrived at the Girl's Charity Worker's meeting at church on Tuesday afternoon, the girls were chatting away like clucking chickens there, too. They wanted to know everything about him. What was he really like? Could I get his autograph? What do your parents think about you running off with an actor?

Mama reminded me that I should have expected this response. After all, Cliff had a good reputation in these parts and the fans adored him. But his reputation was that of a lover boy and an actor, and not the kind of fellow that Adella Lawton ought to be with. Mama also felt that given a little time, this frenzy would pass, and things would get back to normal. I was not so sure. Eunice was right. No matter where we went, given some time, the fans would always be there, at least until he left the stage, if that ever happened.

After the meeting of the Girls Charity Workers where we accomplished nothing, I went to the Club Theater to get some practice time for Friday night's New Year's party, and I really wanted to see if Cliff was still at the theater. I entered the auditorium through the front. I could hear Cliff and others talking behind the stage. I could hear hammering and something that sounded like sawing wood.

"Jesus Christ, what the bloody hell are you trying to do to me, Vic?" It was Cliff's voice.

"Easy does it, English," Vic said. "I just need you to work your magic. You can do it. Show me some of that genius with your saw."

Now was probably not a good time for me to be at the theater. Cliff and Vic were obviously having a moment. I turned to leave and ran into a pair of shoulders and legs, definitely male.

"Hey there, gorgeous! Jimmy McCoy's my name. But you can call me Mick." He sauntered right up to my face like he was going to jump on me.

"Hello, Mr. McCoy, I'm Marie Lawton, pleased to me you." I held out my hand so he would back up.

McCoy grabbed my hand and put one big, wet kiss on the top of it.

"The pleasure's mine." He looked at my piano music and continued to hold my hand. "So are you the sweet piano player dame that everyone's been talking about?"

I heard a voice come from the back of the stage. "Leave her alone, Mick." It was definitely Cliff, who was in a brisk walk in my direction. As usual, his shirt was open, sleeves rolled up, and there was a pencil tucked behind his ear.

"What's up, Cliff? Just trying to introduce myself to this lovely dame here."

"Okay, now leave her alone, Mick," he commanded, obviously perturbed.

"Whoa, Cliff? Am I missing something here? I'm sorry if I am. No need to be hostile." McCoy started backing away from me.

Cliff grabbed my hand, climbed the stairs to the stage, and pulled me toward the back where it was dark. I am sure that Mick saw that move.

He took me in his arms and put his forehead against mine. He liked to do that when he talked to me privately, as if we were the only people in the world. His voice was soft and gentle. "Della, I was wondering when you were going to get here."

This was the first time he ever called me Della. "It's been one of those days...I've missed you, too."

"Are you here to practice?"

"Yes, just a few songs."

"Can you do me a favor when you're done?"

"Anything you want." He looked me in the eyes and smiled. Good thing I could not read his mind on that one.

"What I *need* is for you to help me with the lines to this play." He pulled the playbook for *Thorns and Orange Blossoms* out of his pocket. Our eyes met again. "What I *want* from you is a whole different subject." He paused and smiled to himself. "I knew these lines once. It should take me no time to brush up on them again. Vic's decided to run the first show on Monday night after New Year's, rather than Thursday night. I thought I had a few more days to brush up on this play, and he's changing the set on me at the last minute, so I have that to figure out as well."

"No problem. I can do that," I assured him. "I want to help you all that I can."

"Good, I'll come find you in a bit...see, I knew you'd be good for me." He smiled.

"And Cliff," I said with a smile on my face, "stop flirting with me when I'm at work."

He grinned, touched my face, and walked away in his brisk walk style. "Where'd Mick go?" Cliff yelled.

I heard Mick's voice from the room behind the stage say, "I'm back here with Vic getting my ass chewed again."

"Vic owes me that one with what he has put me through today," he said as he walked back behind the stage.

I had not noticed before, but on the top of the piano was a single red rose.

When I finished playing the piano, we went back to the house to practice lines. Every minute I spent with Cliff, I learned something new about
him, what he liked to eat, where he liked to live, what he liked to wear, how
he loved and protected me, how hard he worked, his constant energy and
zest for life, his abundance of confidence, and even how well he knew his
lines. He had not performed this play in several months. Yet he must have
had a photographic memory because he barely missed one.

After running through the lines once, we had a quiet dinner together
with Eunice.

"Do either of you ever wish that you could settle down in one place
and just run your own business?" This was a real stupid question on my
part.

"This is our business," Eunice said defensively.

"If it does well, we do well. I guess that is why we are all so intense,"
Cliff said.

"More like fanatic." Eunice laughed. Cliff nodded his head in agreement.

"Tell me more about this business," I said to both of them. "How do
you get your bookings?"

Eunice turned to Cliff. "Maybe you ought to answer that question." She
looked at me. "He's quite the student of all of this stuff."

"Well, how we get our bookings has evolved over time. From what I've
read, during the latter part of the nineteenth century, the American theater
system went through several changes. I was not in the business then, but
I understand that theaters outside of the big cities were usually individu-
ally owned and controlled by their owners. The traditional stock system
consisted of a theater with its own stationary group that put on plays and
stayed in one place. This became very expensive and cumbersome for the
theater owner, and downright boring for the audience because they saw the
same people doing the same shows week after week. So eventually there was
a shift to a traveling system, which was made possible by the development
of the railroad across the country.

"So with the traveling companies came the problems associated with
booking these companies in the thousands of theaters that exist across the
country. Bookings were made in a very rudimentary fashion through face-
to-face meetings between theater managers, the traveling performers, and
troupes in Union Square in New York City. Out of this chaotic mess developed the theater circuit, and from that came the booking offices and agents

as we know them today. So we now get our bookings through a booking office that works a particular theater circuit."

"You told me once that you came west because of the Syndicate. What is that all about?"

"You remembered that? Well, the Syndicate was formed around 1896 and basically was a monopoly over theater bookings. I came to this country in 1905 at a time when the Syndicate was in full swing. The Syndicate does not exist today as it did. It has been overrun by the competition of the Shuberts and other theater conglomerates."

"How did that work?" I was curious to hear him talk about the nefarious theater Syndicate.

"Well, the Syndicate got theaters to sign contracts to exclusively book all of their talent and shows through the Syndicate. The contracts spelled out what shows would play, under what conditions and how the money would be handled. The problem was that once a theater was in the Syndicate, the managers could only book their shows with them. The performers had to agree to only perform in Syndicate-controlled theaters. It was an exclusive arrangement all the way around.

"Basically, two guys, Erlanger and Klaw, controlled the whole thing, and they took a good piece of the gross. You can only imagine the effect of this on the smaller theaters. A theater outside of the Syndicate could not get good talent or book quality shows. They had to either join with the Syndicate or get squeezed out. This monopolistic strategy had been happening in other industries in America for some time. It was brilliant the way Erlanger and Klaw employed the same strategy to American Theater. But not so brilliant for the performer, like me.

"Then the Shuberts came along and built a bigger and fiercely competitive organization that I understand eventually may have helped bring the Syndicate down. Everywhere there was a Syndicate Theater, the Shuberts established a competing theater. Even here in Joplin, you have the Shubert Theatre that attracts the prime shows in direct competition with the Club Theater, and it is right down the street. I predict that if the Club Theater remains independent, it will take a beating from the competition. I also predict, as you have heard me say before, that Hollywood will eventually be the death of the traveling troupe as we know it. I kid you not, Della. If you come with me, the life that you would have as a member of a traveling company will likely be very short-lived."

I ignored the suggestion about me going with him on the road. "Where does your company fit into all this? Are you in the Syndicate?"

"We've tried to stay independent. That's probably why I moved around so much. We book with theater managers who have refused to sign on with the Syndicate or the Shuberts, we keep our costs low, our prices lower, we produce good plays, we negotiate lower royalties, and we have been able to compete pretty fairly with the syndicated companies."

Cliff spoke as if he was a college professor. He seemed to have a brilliant understanding of the business and where it was all going. But there was something sad in what he was saying about this business that he loved. He truly believed it was going to end, and soon.

After dinner, we sat together on the couch in the sitting room and ran through his lines again.

"You looked tired, love," he said after we finished the first act.

"Will you take me home? I need to sleep."

"Sure, and then I'm going back to the theater to try to figure out what the stage carpenter is going to do with that set tomorrow."

At home, Mama was awake waiting for me. She was sitting in her favorite chair knitting.

"We've missed having you around here, Marie. Do you think you could manage to get that boy of yours over here for dinner tomorrow?"

I gave her a kiss on the cheek. "Sure, Mama, I will try." Even Mama was beginning to think of Cliff as "that boy of mine." Was I ready to be his? That would mean leaving my home again, leaving my family, leaving my job, not going back to Kansas City, and probably not getting my music degree. But would it mean giving up who I was or wanted to be? Could I even do that? Did Cliff expect me to give up who I wanted to be in order to be with him? Or was he the path to where I wanted to go? He had been the man of my dreams for a while. Could he be that man in real life?

As I lay in my bed, I kept hearing Cliff say his lines over and over again. I loved the way he pronounced his words.

29

On Wednesday, Mama invited Cliff, Vic, Eunice, and anyone else who wanted to come over to supper. Mama and Aunt Maggie spent the whole day cooking. About midday, Eunice joined us and helped. She really did love to cook, too. The boys thoroughly enjoyed my Mama's home cooking and were looking forward to a real home-cooked meal. My finishing school training came in handy because I set the most beautiful candle-lit table in the dining room using Mama's *Haviland* china dishes.

They all showed up about six, even McCoy. He couldn't stop apologizing to me for being so forward. We had a lovely meal of roast goose and apple stuffing. Aunt Maggie made her famous cornbread. Papa contributed several bottles of wine.

When it was over, everyone helped clean up, then thanked Mama profusely, and excused themselves to go back to the theater. Cliff gave me a hug and a kiss and was gone. Eunice stayed with Mama and me. She wanted to learn how to knit, so Eunice watched Mama while she knitted a simple scarf.

On Thursday at nine in the morning, Jenkins had summoned me for a short meeting to go over the schedule for the next week. He was all business and said nothing to me about my relationship with Cliff.

After Jenkins was finished, I walked over to the piano. There was a rose and a note on my piano. The note was written by Cliff in the most artistically exquisite handwriting:

My Dearest Della: I hope this note finds you well. Please thank your mother and Maggie from all of us for the most delicious meal. The ladies have arrived today, Thursday, and so have the costumes, etc. We are all going to help the ladies move into their house, and then there will be much work getting the costumes organized. I expect we will do a quick read through of the play tonight. I do not expect to be home before 10:00 p.m. If I do not see you today, please know that you are in my heart. Love, Cliff.

The entire group of dinner guests sent Mama a bouquet of daisies with a card that said, *Thank you from your hungry servants, VDESC.* Along with the card were four tickets to the first show. Mama and Aunt Maggie were especially delighted.

As the day passed, I began to miss Cliff as I wondered what he was doing and who he was with. What a ninny. One day without him and I was beginning to panic. I remembered when he told me that he would not let one day go by without seeing me. Now, this day was slipping by, and we were likely not going to see each other. Maybe I could go to him if he wasn't going to come to me. I could go to the house tonight and wait for him to come home. I wanted to surprise him, for once.

Joe offered to take me to the theater in the buggy. From there, I walked to Cliff's house on Byers Street. It was dark as I reached up to knock on the door. No one answered. The front door was slightly open, so I quietly stepped into the house. As if on cue, Cliff came running down the stairs with his shirt off and a towel over his shoulders that he used to dry his wet hair. When he saw me, his eyes lit up and he smiled.

"I was hoping it was you knocking on the front door." He came down the stairs and took me in his arms. His face was smooth, and he smelled like soap.

"Hello, you," I said. "I couldn't let this day go by without seeing you."

"Sounds like you are catching what I have," he whispered in my ear. "Let me get some clothes on, and we can go have a drink or just sit here and talk, whatever you want." He turned to walk back up the stairs.

"I want to come with you."

"Della," he started shaking his head. "Not a good idea." He looked up as if he was trying to determine if anyone else was in the house.

"I just want to see your room." He hesitated but didn't fight me. He just gave me his hand and pulled me up the stairs behind him.

Cliff's room was located in the back of the house. He slowly opened the door and let me walk into the room first. It was a large room with a four-post bed and a curved alcove that looked out over the backyard garden. There were two comfortable matching burgundy chairs facing each other and an exquisite walnut table in the alcove. The room was decorated in deep maroon or burgundy, very masculine. The floor was hardwood with lovely Persian rugs scattered about. Cliff went right to his walk-in closet looking for something to wear, and then with shirt in hand, he left the room again.

I slowly looked around his room and noticed a gun in a holster hanging from a hook on the wall by the closet. On his dresser there were some papers, along with a photograph of a young and very attractive woman. She had autographed the photo, *"Cliff, I love you always. Betty."* There was another small photo on the dresser of Cliff with one of his traveling companies. On one side, Cliff, who was wearing a suit and derby, stood with a couple women and men. On the other side was an older man with a suitcase and a pipe in his hand. This must have been very early stock or Vaudeville.

Next to the bed on the nightstand was another photo of a woman in a small frame. I looked closer and saw that it was a photo of me sitting at the piano smiling. It must have been taken when he was here before with Garside's Company.

The table in the alcove was piled high with play scripts waiting to be read. There was another pile of sheet music and several novels. His bed was neatly made and looked like it had never been slept in. On the floor were two large black trunks. Clothes were hung neatly in the closet, and his shoes were arranged in perfect order on the floor.

Cliff came back in the room with a shirt on. I looked at him and smiled as he buttoned his shirt.

"Anything else you want to see?"

"That picture, who is Betty?" I pointed to the frame beauty.

"Betty is my little sister. She's still in England."

"She is very lovely," I said with relief that Betty was not an old girlfriend.

"She is very special to me. I would like to bring her to America some-day. She is studying to be a nurse."

"I saw the picture on the nightstand."

"That is a picture of a very dear friend of mine." He smiled, walked toward me, and took me in his arms. "Della, you really shouldn't be in my bedroom," he whispered. "But I like that you are here."

"I feel safe here," I could only whisper. "Kiss me."

He did kiss me long and hard like we had been apart for a long time.

"Della, Della, Della." He was whispering again. "I love you so...when are you going to tell me that you will come with me? I want you in my room every night." His hands were holding my face, and he peered into my eyes.

"I want to be with you every night and every day, too."

"No, I sense that you are holding back. You are not sure of all of this yet, are you?"

"I am sure of how I feel about you."

"And how is that?"

"I want to be with you." I knew he wanted to hear something more from me.

"That's a good starting point. Is there something you are not sure about?"

"I would be leaving my life as I know it to come with you and be in your life. That is all." I felt immature and terribly indecisive at that moment.

He was silent for a moment. "That is a good reason to be dubious. I understand how difficult this is for you. I had to make a similar life-altering decision once. But I want you to know that you would be going to a place where you belong and where you are loved. Do you know that?"

I had to find the courage to say the words, to give him the assurance he needed from me. "I just need time...but Cliff," I reached my hand to his face, "I do love you." He smiled and gazed into my eyes. I know he had been waiting to hear those words, and I guess I had been waiting for the right time to say them.

30

There was an open party at the Club Theater on New Year's Eve, 1915, which included a catered dinner. I was the entertainment for the dinner hour. Jenkins wanted me to play soft piano music. Then a small orchestra took over, and there would be dancing. I had to work for about an hour and half, and then I was free to mingle. Cliff did not plan to come to the party until much later because he had so much preparation for the show. I wore a new dress that night made of taupe satin, with a high neck lace collar and fringe trim. It was something Olive had picked out for one of my performance dresses when I was in Kansas City. I must have looked enchanting because I received a lot of compliments and attention from the men at the party. Even Albert Jones stopped by the piano to say hello and wish me a Happy New Year.

"Hey there, beautiful," Albert said as he walked up to the piano.

"Albert, how are you?" I extended my hand. He took it and held on longer than I had anticipated.

"You know, I'm hearing talk about you?"

"Talk?" I slowly pulled my hand away.

"They say you're running around with some actor from the company that's going to play here this season. True?

"Running around?"

"Adella, you know what I mean. Just don't go throwing your life away over some two-bit actor."

"Albert, I'm not throwing my life away. I have friends here—that's all." I was not up to talking to Albert about my relationship with Cliff. "And he's not some two-bit actor."

"You belong with someone that's going to treat you right."

"Well, there's no one here in Joplin like that for me."

"You never know. There sure as heck could be."

I was not sure where this conversation was going. "Where's your Susan?" I looked through the crowd.

"She's at the table, with my parents." His eyes met mine, and he just stood there for a moment ever so silent as if he was searching for an answer from me.

"Well, listen, Albert, I have to get started here. Perhaps we can talk about this another time."

"Yes, okay, sure." He kissed my cheek and walked away. I was not going to think about Albert right now, and I couldn't let his words go to my head and ruin my concentration. It was my time to perform.

The dinner hour went well, but I didn't get much time to eat. There were a lot of people I knew at dinner, and the champagne kept coming my way. So by the time I finished serenading the crowd, I was feeling pretty happy, or maybe a better word for it is fuzzy. A group of people entered the room, women and men. I recognized Vic and Eunice, right away. Vic was in a grey wool suit, and Eunice wore a black evening dress that looked stunning on her. Jimmy McCoy was in the group, along with two other men. One was probably Orrin Burke. But I had not yet met any of the other Van Dyke Eaton performers. There were three women with them, and they were all beautifully dressed for the evening with their hair looking perfectly coiffed. They took a table toward the back of the room and probably hoped, if they were anything like Cliff, that they would not be recognized.

When I left the piano, I slowly made my way back to their table, meeting and greeting everyone I knew and some that I didn't, along the way. Vic and Eunice both stood when I approached the table and walked toward me smiling.

"Are you finished for the night?" Eunice said after exchanging hugs.

"I am. Where's Cliff?"

"Oh, he'll be around. I'm surprised English is not here already 'cause you're here," Vic said.

"Introduce me to the ladies, Vic."

"Sure," he said as he placed his hand on the small of my back and walked me to the table. "Ladies, this is Miss Lawton...Cliff's Miss Lawton...you may call her Marie.

"Marie, this is Bessie Jackson, Mary Enos, and Helen DeLand." I took each of their hands one by one and greeted them personally. They all seemed quite pleasant. "This is Orrin Burke, and of course, you know McCoy." I offered my hand to Orrin, and of course, Mick gave my hand a kiss and winked at me. He was sitting next to Bessie Jackson, and I am sure she noticed that wink. She studied my face.

"I'm looking forward to see your performance," I said.

"As we, yours. We understand you know your way around a piano," Bessie replied. The others nodded their heads in agreement. Now I was not quite sure how I felt sitting here looking at the women that Cliff spent so much time with on and off stage. They all were uniquely glamorous. He could be with any one of them. This was awkward for me, but I did not want to give off even the slightest indication of that.

I whispered to Vic, "I'm a bit flushed. I do need to get some air."

"Do you want company?" Vic said.

"Oh no, please. I'll be right back," I graciously said to the ladies at the table.

I made my way back through the crowd down the stairs to the auditorium. There was a stage door in the back where I could get a quick breath of cool air. It was the very door where Cliff and I first spoke that summer he was here. As I was walking back to the door, I heard someone jump up on the stage and come running up behind me. Cliff, appearing out of thin air, was dressed in a black formal suit with tails and a white shirt with a tie and looked so handsome.

"Della, where you going, love?" He picked me up in his arms and swung me around. "Happy New Year's Eve."

"Happy New Year's Eve to you, too. I thought you would never get here," I whispered.

"I was hoping to grab you as my dance partner and show off some of the steps I learned from Fred Astaire. Where are you off to?"

"I'm feeling a little warm from the champagne, I haven't eaten, and I need some air, Cliff. I'll be right back." I started to pull away.

"No, hey, hold up…take me with you." He followed me out of the stage door, as the cool night air hit my warm flushed face and felt wonderful.

"You look beautiful, Della." He took hold of my shoulders and pulled my back against him as he leaned on the wall. He wrapped his arms around the front of me and pulled me back to lean against him. The stars were out. "Just lean back here and relax a minute. Let the cool air refresh you." His voice was hypnotic. I gently relaxed against him.

"I am so happy I get to be here with you for the next twelve weeks."

"Yes and before you know it you're going to be on your way to the next town and the next theater."

He was quiet for a moment.

"Of course, you will be with me."

"I will?"

"Yes. You'll play piano and even perform in the plays with me. We'll travel and see a lot of different places."

"How would I live without a job?"

"You don't have to worry about that, love. I have plenty of money for both of us to live. Someday, when the time is right and the place is right, we'll settle down, I'll buy us a house and maybe even have a family. We would be married, of course." He spoke as if he was dreaming out loud.

"I would like to have children, someday."

"Then it sounds like a good plan."

"It still sounds like an impossible dream to me."

"I was afraid you would see it that way."

It was quiet again. But I needed to bring this up.

"Cliff, have you been with other women?"

"Della, I'm twenty-eight years old, and I haven't exactly been a hermit."

"And your relationship didn't work out with those other women?"

"I would not exactly call what I had a relationship."

"What makes you think it will work out for us?"

"I don't have a crystal ball. I just know it's different with you. I haven't wanted a relationship with any other women. But with you, I really want to make us work. You have to trust me on that." It was silent again. "What about you, Della, do you want to experience other men?"

"I have experienced other men."

"You have?" He was visibly taken aback.

"Not in that way...I have never experienced loving a man, until you." He gently kissed my hair. "Would it make a difference to you if I had been with another man?"

"I'd be jealous as hell." He had a pained expression on his face.

"Well, now you know how I feel."

"Come here." He turned me around to face him and pulled me in closer so I could feel the entire length of his body. He was so warm and smelled so good. Our eyes met, and his lips crushed into mine. Every nerve in my body came alive. I reached up and ran my hands through the back of his hair so he would not pull away. He put his forehead to mine. "Della, Della...I want you so bad. I could take you home right now, and we could be alone together, but," he paused. "I can't do that with you. If we're going to do this, we must do this right."

I said nothing for fear that whatever I'd say would be the wrong thing.

Then I pressed my lips to his and kissed him again. He pulled back abruptly and put his forehead to mine again. His eyes were closed. His fingers lightly traced my chin and went down my throat. All I could hear was Cliff breathing and the dim sound of dance music coming from the theater. Every once in a while, I could hear the breeze as it moved through the trees and bushes outside the theater. We must have stood like that for several minutes. All of the issues that stood in the way of us being together seemed to fade away.

"Della, I have a feeling that 1916 is going to be a memorable year for you and I. So you know what we're going to do? We're going to go in there and dance ourselves into 1916." Cliff grabbed my arm and pulled me through the door to the dance floor where a lot of couples were dancing. We melted into the crowd.

31

*To laugh often and much; to win the respect of intelligent people
and the affection of children; to earn the appreciation of honest
critics and endure the betrayal of false friends; to appreciate
beauty; to find the best in others; to leave the world a little better
place than we found it, whether by a healthy child, a garden
patch or a redeemed social condition; to know even one life
breathed easier because you lived. This is to have succeeded.*

~WALT WHITMAN (1819-1892)

My New Year's resolution was simple. I wanted to figure out the rest of my life, especially if I would have a life with Cliff. There was still way too much that I didn't know about him. He wanted me to leave the stability of my home and go on the road with him, and I barely knew him. Simple? An easy decision? Who was I kidding?

We were able to get three dances in at the Club before people started to recognize my dance partner. We were having great fun dancing together and blending into the crowd, but before we knew it, women started to crowd around him and ask for autographs on the "New Year's at the Club" napkins. I retreated to the table with Vic and Eunice. Vic was quick to assure me that Cliff knew how to handle the crowd and that he would get away before too long. Eunice looked at me with a glint in her eyes and said, *"You better get used to this, honey."* It was as if she was saying, *"What did I tell you?"*

Hell, what did I expect? The townsfolk cherished him. It wasn't just the single women who crowded him. Olive had warned me to watch out for the lonely married ladies, who were always looking for some young, available man to suit their needs. When Cliff did finally break away, he came over to the table and grabbed my arm.

"Bloody hell, I really enjoyed that!" he whispered to Vic sarcastically.

"Can't take the heat, lover boy?"

"No, I told them all they had the wrong guy. That Hastings was over at the table, the cute guy with the black suit." Cliff pointed at McCoy.

"The hell you did," McCoy laughed.

"Della, love, it is time for us to go. Let's go and see your father. Maybe I'll get some peace there."

We ended up spending New Year's at the Criterion with my family. The other Van Dyke & Eaton performers followed us there as well. Papa set up a special table at the back of the saloon where we could sit, drink, and play cards. The busy saloon was filled with smoke, talk, and laughter. Cliff sat in the back with me and the other members of the company, unrecognizable under one of Papa's caps. He had taken off his coat and tie and loosened the buttons on his shirt. He even rolled up his sleeves. At one point when Papa got real busy, Cliff got behind the bar with him as his assistant bartender. I could tell he enjoyed being able to freely mingle without being bothered or asked for his autograph.

As the night wore on, Cliff and Vic became more animated. Before I knew it, they were acting out various Vaudeville scenarios. The scenes were quite moronic, but their timing was impeccable. Sometimes Cliff played the straight man, and Vic played the fool. One of the funniest was the cop arresting the drunk. Vic knew how to be drunk. Cliff, with his British accent, played a great straight man, the cop.

Cliff: Sir, say your name.
Vic: Your name.
Cliff: No, I mean <u>say</u> your name.
Vic: I mean <u>say</u> your name.
Cliff: Sir, are you trying to make a fool out of me?
Vic: It's too late. I dare say, bobbie, you're already a fool.
Cliff: How dare you call me a foul name?
Vic: (Aside) I called him a fool, not a fowl.
Cliff: Sir, I'm going to arrest you.
Vic: What's the charge officer?
Cliff: Drunk and disorderly.
Vic: No, I mean what's the charge?
Cliff: I said drunk and disorderly.
Vic: Officer, are you trying to make a fool of me?
Cliff: Why do you say that?
Vic: Officer, why won't you answer my question?
Cliff: Which question is that?
Vic: The question that I asked you.
Cliff: Why do you ask so many questions?
Vic: Well, if the charge is more than $2.00, I don't have the money.
Cliff: The money for what?
Vic: To pay the charge.
Cliff: Are you offering a bribe, sir?
Vic: No, I'm offering to pay the charge.
Cliff: What charge?
Vic: I asked you that first.
Cliff: I don't know what charge you are talking about, sir.
Vic: If you don't know the charge, officer, why are you arresting me?

The crowd in the Criterion was rolling in laughter, and these guys never broke character for a minute, as they continued performing short comedy sketches taking the folks in the saloon beyond Joplin to a place they all could enjoy.

32

Everyone hears what you say. Friends listen to what you say; best friends listen to what you don't say.

~UNKNOWN

Olive was expected home on the Sunday following New Year's Day. Her train arrived at about dinnertime. She was going to be here for two weeks before her next semester started. I figured she would be exceedingly busy with her family at first since she missed the Christmas holiday with them. Olive and I really needed to spend time together.

Cliff had been tied up in rehearsals on New Year's Day, and we had, as he forewarned me, very little time together. I was not needed at the Club until Monday morning. On Sunday, Papa, Mama, and I went to church. I had to sing in the choir. After church, I went to the church reception, as usual. It was probably a good idea for me to go through these motions just to assure everyone in church that I wasn't about to elope with that *actor*.

A group of inquisitive church ladies, whom I barely knew, approached me at the reception in the basement. "Where is your young man?" one of them asked.

"Oh, you mean Mr. Priest? He really isn't *my* young man. Just a friend." I tried to smile and be polite.

"Well, he's been coming to church with you. Is he here today, Miss Marie?"

"Well," I repeated, "he is hard at work on the opening show." They were just being nosy.

"You know, Marie, those young actors don't stay in one place too long," another one said.

My frustration was beginning to show. "No, especially when people are always so bothersome with them."

I kept thinking about Albert's words, *"running around with some actor."* He made it sound so cheap and immoral. As my frustration grew, I found my way to the piano in the great sanctuary and spent the next two hours playing Rachmaninov, over and over again, trying to empty my mind, but thinking only of my relationship with *that actor.*

That evening, I met Olive at the train station. Mr. Crockett had stopped to pick me up in his Model T on his way to get her. We made small talk on the way to the station. I think Mr. Crockett knew not to bring up my relationship with that *actor*, but he sure had a gift for talking around the *actor.*

"Are you enjoying your work at the Club?"

"Yes, very much so."

"Do the people there treat you right?"

"Mostly, sir."

"Are you planning on going back to Kansas City with Olive?"

"I don't know, sir. I would like to continue my education."

"You know, in life it seems things happen sometimes to get you off course. But I like to look at it another way. It may not seem so at the time, but I think things happen to right your sails…set you on a course. That's what I think. Mebbe I think too much." He chuckled.

"That's a fresh way to look at life, sir."

Thank God, Olive's train was on time for once. She was surprised and happy to see me.

"Della, I have missed you," she said as she gave me a hug.

"You look wonderful," I told her, as I realized a part of me wished I could have stayed in Kansas City with her and another part of me wished I could go back to Kansas City with her when she left.

"When can we spend time together?" she asked as her father loaded her bags into the car.

"I have to work tomorrow morning at the Club. I have a rehearsal, and then the show opens tomorrow, Monday, night. The next show isn't until Thursday.

"Do you have time now? Can you come back to my house?"

"Sure, now would be a good time."

The ride to Olive's house was a pleasant one. She was chattering like crazy about Kansas City and all of the fun that I had been missing. Her whole family was waiting for her in the drive when we arrived at her house. She had two younger brothers, Stephen and Maxwell, a younger sister, Muriel, and of course, her mother, Charlotte, who was one of my favorite people.

After Olive had greeted her family, she and I went into her room to unpack her trunk and talk. She wasted no time getting to the point. "Tell me everything about Mr. Hastings."

"There's not much to tell."

"I don't buy that for a minute, Della."

"Well, he is busy in rehearsals now and will be for the rest of the season. Then he goes on to St. Joseph, Missouri, and then to Dubuque, Iowa."

"He asked you to go with him, right? Are you going with him?"

"He didn't exactly ask me. He said I could go with him if I wanted. I don't think I can."

"What does that mean?"

"It wouldn't be the right thing for me to do. I have a job here in Joplin, and I do want to get back to school in Kansas City when that is done. They're talking about closing the Club down for remodeling in the spring, and maybe then I'll just come back to Kansas City."

"Della, do you love him?"

"I'm so crazy about him, I cannot think straight."

"Then go with him."

"Albert thinks I would be throwing my life away on an actor."

"Albert? How did Albert ever get involved in this?"

"He approached me at the Club. He said he heard talk that I had been running around with an actor, and he didn't like it. He told me not to waste my life."

"You know what I think? I think Albert needs to stay the hell out of this." She grabbed my shoulders and peered into my eyes. "You are not his business. This is about you and a man who loves you and, on top of all that, a man who offers you a pretty exciting life."

"A pretty difficult life."

"A pretty amazing life compared to life in Joplin. Della, no path you choose in life is easy. There are always going to be issues that have to be dealt with and problems that have to be solved. The question is, do you want to go through life with the man you love, even if he presents more of a challenge, or do you want to spend your life on easy street with someone you don't really love, bored out of your mind and wondering what the man you love is doing?"

"What if Albert is right? What if Cliff isn't what he appears to be and this thing for each other ends up being a total flop?"

"No, no, no. What if Cliff is all that he professes to be, and what if you don't go with him and you both end up terribly brokenhearted? What if you never find another person that you feel this way about? What if you always wished that you had tried to make it work with him, that you had given him a chance? What about those '*What ifs*'?"

"Olive, it has only been since Christmas Eve. I need to think about this. I need time. It's a major decision for me, and I'm not even sure if we'll have the same feelings for each other by the end of the season. He may not want to take me with him by then. I will not, cannot make this decision now."

"Della, this *thing* with you two has been going on a lot longer than Christmas Eve. Come to think of it, I've never met him. Can I meet him? I'll be able to tell right away if he's good for you."

"You can, and you will meet him. But don't go judging him like that. It doesn't matter. It's how I feel about the life that he has chosen. That is the issue."

Olive's father took me home. It was about nine in the evening. Papa was still at the saloon, and I expect Mama was with him. My aunt and uncle must have been asleep.

When we arrived home, Cliff was sitting on the back stoop waiting for me. I thanked Mr. Crockett and quickly walked up to Cliff.

"Hi there, stranger," I jovially said.

"Hey, you. I sure am glad to see you. Thought maybe you wouldn't ever come home," he said as he stood and took both of my hands.

"I've been visiting Olive, but I would have been here sooner if I'd known you were here."

"Can you sit with me out here for a bit?"

We both sat down on the stoop. "You look tired," I said.

"I am beat." He was still holding my hands. His face was pale, and his eyes were droopy.

"You need a good night's sleep."

"Not without seeing you first."

"How is the show going?"

"It's coming along, should be a good opener."

"Can I get you something? Thirsty?"

"Nope." He put his arm around me and pulled me against him. We sat there together looking out at the stars. "I just want to sit here in the quiet of the night with you."

33

Silence is Golden.
~UNKNOWN

Monday was a hectic day. I had a short specialties rehearsal in the morning with Cliff, which went very well. When it was over, we had a minute to talk.

"Well done," he said lightly touching my shoulder. "When are you due back here?" he asked.

"Not until six, with show time at seven. How are you feeling?"

"I'm feeling pretty good. I'm ready to get this show on the road. Lord Randolph has gotten under my skin, so to speak."

"Well, Lord Randolph, I am sure your performance will be smashingly good."

"It'll be better once we get into the full swing of things and I don't have the time to be tired of it all." I didn't realize that Cliff got tired of it all.

"Do you get a break today?"

"Actually, yes. I do not expect to be here much past two this afternoon. Do you want to meet for dinner and come to the theater together? I could come by and get you around four?"

"Hey, Cliff, please. You don't need to worry about entertaining me. You should get some rest this afternoon."

"What if I told you that it would be better for me to have some time with you today?"

Jenkins walked into the room and was watching us from the back of the auditorium. We both noticed him at about the same time.

"I'll see you at four," I told him. Cliff grabbed his pencil and scribbled something on a piece of paper. He handed me the note, turned and walked back up to the stage.

The *Thorns and Orange Blossoms* cast was beginning to assemble on the stage. It was time for me to make an exit so I could read the note without Jenkins staring me down. Outside the theater, I tore it open to find Cliff had written, *"Remember, I love you and miss you. Cliff."*

When I arrived home, there was a long box waiting for me. It had no name on it, and Mama claimed to have had no idea where it came from. The box appeared to be from a store in St. Louis. Intrigued by this box, I opened it. There was a card, which read, *"Here's to a great winter season together."* Love, *Cliff.* I tore open the paper to find a beautiful teal blue satin dress with light teal sequins and creamy colored lace. It was my size. The collar was open, the sleeves were long, and the skirt was floor-length.

Two days ago, I had no idea what to wear on my opening night. Cliff took care of that for me. This dress was perfectly exquisite. The teal blue looked amazingly wonderful with my blue eyes. Cliff was so busy running from rehearsal to rehearsal, but he still found the time to do this for me. He was one of the most thoughtful people I had ever known. And even though it was his job to go pretend he was someone else, to pretend he loved someone else, he did not pretend when it came to me.

Cliff seemed to have so little. He told me he traveled light. Every material thing that he owned was in his room. Whenever I would ask him what I could get for him, he would say, "Just give me a smile."

The Monday night show was sensational, and the audience loved Cliff and Bessie Jackson in the lead roles. By Tuesday, he started running his lines for the next play, *The Squaw Man* even though he had four more shows of *Thorns and Orange Blossoms* to give. We sat together reading this play alone in the living room of the house. He knew most of the lines for the part of John Roseleigh, which did not surprise me.

"You know, Della, you read these parts very well. You really belong on the stage," Cliff said as he reached for my hand.

"If that is my destiny, I can only hope I figure it out someday soon," I replied thoughtfully. The room was quiet but for the ticking sound of the grandfather clock in the front hallway. It felt good to sit in the quiet room with him and do nothing but read through the play or just stare at the ceiling. I was content to be near him holding his hand in silence. It reminded me of the bright red post card that Cliff had in his scrapbook that read, *"Silence is Golden."* Our quiet moments together were our treasured moments.

"Have you given much more thought to what you want to do when this season ends?" Cliff asked. We both had avoided this topic of conversation for a while.

"Cliff, do you believe in destiny? Do you think we were destined to meet?"

"I believe there is a logical order to the universe and that we are part of each other's logical order. I guess you can call that destiny. And, think about it. If I hadn't come along the creek when I did and if I hadn't been the kind of person that I am, a bit daft and pretty skilled at knocking people off their feet, I hate to think what could have happened to you." Our eyes met for a split second. Then he went back to reading.

I knew that Cliff was a Mason and he wore a gold Masonic ring, sometimes. He was wearing it today. It rubbed against my fingers when he held my hand. But we never talked about what all of that meant to him. There was a newspaper article in the scrapbook that Eunice had that reported Cliff had lost the ring. The article, which was in Eunice's category of *why did they even print this article,* read,

> *A gold ring inlaid with a Masonic emblem lay on the sidewalk on Moody Street, about opposite the public library, for more than four hours Saturday night. The ring was dropped by Clifford Hastings, leading man of the Adam Good Stock Company, on his way to the Scenic Theatre. He pulled a bunch of keys from his pocket and heard something drop but thought it was a penny and passed on. It was not until after the second act of the play that Mr. Hastings discovered that it was his ring that he had*

> *dropped. He then made up his mind that the ring was gone for good. After the play Mr. Hastings and Harry Vickery went over to Moody Street to search for the ring but with little hopes of finding it, as it was then nearly eleven o'clock and the ring had been lost about seven o'clock. But much to the surprise of both men, the ring was there and Mr. Hastings was very happy over recovering it.*

I was curious about the ring. "Why is that ring so important to you?" He looked at me as if to say *'where did that question come from'?*

"It's not the ring that is important. It is what the ring signifies that is important."

"What does is signify?"

He thought for a moment and then said, "My work to become a better person, to understand my life better, and how best to relate to the people in this country that has become my home."

"Is that why you became a Mason?"

"It was a way for me to become connected when I first came to America. I knew no one and had nothing. In a way, becoming a Mason probably saved my life. I was a foreigner in a strange land. There were a lot of knowledgeable and important people in this country connected to the Masons. So I thought this would be a good thing for me. It keeps me grounded. It gives me a way to give back something meaningful."

"Is being a Mason like a religion? Do you believe in God?"

"Of course I believe in God, but probably not in the same way as you have been taught in your church. The Masons accept all beliefs in a higher power. I accept the philosophy of a God, but I am not hung up on the fable. God is more scientific than that and I follow more scientific thought and analysis. Life is a blessing, death is the end and when I die I do not want there to be a lot of grieving and ceremony. Death is just the natural progression of my life."

I didn't want to think or talk about his death so I changed the subject. "You were missed at church on Sunday."

"Oh, I was?"

"People have noticed us and they are talking."

"What are they saying?"

"Some like us together, and others...well others think I would be crazy in the head to run off with you."

He laughed.

"I expect as much. Guess which ones I'm voting for."

34

Really great people make you feel that you, too, can become great.
~MARK TWAIN (1835-1910)

On Friday night, Olive came to the show. She had never met Cliff and she wanted to make sure they met before she went back to Kansas City on Sunday. After the show she met me at the piano when everyone else was in the reception area greeting people and signing autographs.

"It was a lovely show, Della. I don't think I have ever heard you play the piano so well." I gave her a hug.

"You know," I said, "I could get used to having your cheerful self around me."

"I loved the part at the end where Cliff gets reunited with his wife. He gave Bessie Jackson a pretty good kiss. Does that bother you? His love for her was pretty convincing to me."

"It's not supposed to bother me. But it still does, a little." I saw Cliff briskly walking toward us from the back of the auditorium.

"Hey there, you two. You must be Olive." Cliff extended his hand. Olive gave him a hug much to his surprise. "I am so very pleased to make your acquaintance," Cliff said, smiling as he took Olive's hand and gave it a light kiss. Then, he wrapped both of his arms around me and gave me a big hug lifting me off the ground. "How is my best girl?" It happened so fast, he did not miss a beat. "What would you ladies like to do? Do you want to go have a drink somewhere or a bite to eat?"

Olive looked at him, shook her head yes, but was somewhat speechless for a few seconds. She was not used to someone with so much energy at this time of night.

"You've got to give me a few minutes. Can we walk over to the house? I'll get cleaned up and get this makeup off of my face. Then I'm all yours." He was certainly cheerful, which meant that he thought the play went pretty well.

So Olive and I walked with Cliff to his house. We sat in the front room while Cliff went upstairs. McCoy and Burke came in and shuffled upstairs. Vic and Eunice were next. After we finished our introductions, Vic went upstairs, while Eunice went to the kitchen to make tea. She wanted us to stay and visit with them. She lightly touched my arm. "Forget going out. Stay with the rest of us," she said.

"Maybe we will." I smiled at her.

I decided to softly play some classical music, while Olive sat on a chair by the piano.

When Cliff came downstairs, his hair was wet and he had obviously cleaned up. He smelled better than a lilac bush in full bloom. I just wanted to bury my face into his neck, which was probably not something a respectable young lady should do, but I certainly could imagine it. Eunice brought us tea while Cliff and Olive sat on each of the winged-back chairs facing each other and I continued playing the piano. They were quietly talking, and I needed to let them get to know one another, my two favorite people.

"So you're the fellow that has stolen my best friend's heart?" Olive said to Cliff as she sipped her tea.

"Oh, I wish that were true," he said.

I smiled to myself. Cliff pretended not to know how I felt about him.

"Well, I think she is very lucky that you found her, again. Maybe you can show her the world. She is so talented. She doesn't belong here without you in Joplin."

Eunice brought in a bottle of wine and glasses for each of us. She handed a filled wine glass to each of us and then left the room again.

"Maybe you would have better luck encouraging her to make the move. My powers of persuasion have not worked with her," he said as he smiled his adoring smile.

"What are you two doing talking about me behind my back?" I interrupted.

"How is that behind your back when you are over there listening to every word we say?" Olive replied.

"It sounds as though you have forgotten that I am in the room."

"There is very little chance that I would ever forget that you are in a room with me, my dear." Cliff stood and walked over to the piano. He sat on the bench and put his arm around me. He leaned over, kissed my hair, and whispered, "I adore you." Then Cliff turned and said to Olive, "Your friend needs time because if she comes with me, it will be a major change in her lifestyle. I respect that. She would not have a permanent home like she has now, or a job, and she would have to travel much lighter than she is used to traveling. This house, it is an anomaly. We are usually in one room in a boardinghouse. No kitchen, and sometimes the bath facilities are quite primitive. Our time in one place is for the most part quite short. You no sooner get your bearings with the town, and you're moving again. And there is no assurance that the company will even stay together beyond next summer. I fear I am too used to living this way. It can be a brutal life for someone who is not used to it."

I listened intently trying to picture myself in his world. No matter how hard I tried, I couldn't make it work.

"It sounds exciting to me," Olive said.

"I fear the glamour of what we do for a living is overrated. Della tells me that you are studying to be a teacher, a literature teacher."

He was a master at changing the subject. It seemed as if he sensed my discomfort with the discussion about his world, especially when I said nothing.

"Yes, I love English literature and contemporary American authors, as well. I should be ready to teach after a few more semesters in school."

"We should have you help us select our next plays." He chuckled. "You know, you and I are not much different in what we do. For me to perform a play, it is always useful to read the novel, if there happens to be a novel. I analyze the plot much like you probably do, and I try to get into the mind of the character that I am playing."

Cliff and Olive continued to talk about literature. It was obvious to me that he was knowledgeable about this subject probably because of all of the plays that he had performed. It was also obvious to me that Cliff had found a dear friend in Olive.

When we were alone in the room, Olive spoke.

"I don't care what they say about you running off with *an actor*, this man is the real thing, and I hope you realize it before it's too late."

When Vic, Cliff, and Eunice returned to the room, Eunice had more wine.

"I am excited to say that we might have a handle on the next schedule of plays," Vic announced.

"What do you have in mind?" Cliff asked.

"It's nothing that should come as a shock to you," Vic said.

"Let's have it," Cliff said.

"First, we'll do *Ishmael*, with Cliff in the lead of course. Then, I think we will do *The Embezzler*, *Out of the Fold*, Broadhurst's *The Man of the Hour*, *Lena Rivers*, *In Panama*, and *St. Elmo*. I'm just not yet sure about the order. I think we may close with *Kathleen Mavourneen*, which makes a total of twelve plays in twelve weeks."

"The novel *Ishmael* by Emma Dorothy Eliza Nevitte Southworth is one of the widely read books of our time," Olive said. "I wish I was going to be here to see that."

"Geez, Louise, her name is a mouthful," I said. "Olive, you should try and come home for that show."

"Ishmael is one of my favorite parts, maybe because it tracks my own life story to a point. You have the boy, Ishmael Worth, in this life struggle of shame, poverty, and even fate itself, only to rise above it all and become one of the best legal minds of the country. The rising above it all is where the similarities to my life end."

"Oh, I'm not so sure about that," Eunice interrupted. "You have risen above a lot, old chap." Eunice was always quick to champion Cliff.

"What other parts will you play, Cliff?" Olive asked.

She must have been reading my mind. Olive was interested in learning which plays were based on the literary works of our time. Everyone was silent as Cliff told the stories of the people he would become over the next few months.

"In the *Embezzler*, I play a district attorney. I really enjoy this part. Maybe I would do well to quit acting and start practicing law," Cliff said with a grin.

I could not help but think of Albert, and I must have frowned because Cliff gave me a funny look.

"*Out of the Fold* is another love story, written by Langdon McCormick. This play was first produced in 1904 at the American Theatre on 42nd Street in New York City. We first did this play at the American, but we were not the first cast. I play a schoolmaster by the name of Nolan Crane who falls in love with a young woman, Helene, with a past that she is hiding from the world. McCoy is the villain in this one. He also is in love with Helene.

"In *Man of the Hour*, I play, Alwyn Bennett, a well-to-do young man without much direction in life. He gets elected mayor and opposes the local political men who set out to destroy him. Unfortunately, he is also in love with one of their nieces, Dallas Wainright, played by Bessie. And so the drama unfolds…how to achieve one's political goals without destroying the one you love. This is one of Broadhurst's better plays first produced in 1906."

Olive was listening intently and nodding her head in recognition of the authors and plays.

"In *Lena Rivers*, which is based upon the famous novel by Mary Holmes, I play another lover boy by the name of Durward Bellmont. He is caught in a drama between the girl he loves, Lena Rivers, and her cousin, Caroline, who, out of jealousy, wants to destroy the relationship between Bellmont and Lena. It turns out that Bellmont's stepfather is Lena's long lost father which gives this play a rather interesting twist.

"I play a musician in *In Panama*, who holds '*love as a detriment to art and marriage as a blight to both, but the God, money, above all.*' Bessie plays the part of a heroic sister to McCoy, who plays the embezzling clerk. This drama definitely has several twists and turns.

"*St. Elmo* is based upon the popular novel by Augusta Jane Evans written in 1866. I am none other than St. Elmo Murray. Edna Earle, again played by Bessie, is an orphan taken in by my wealthy mother following a train wreck. We develop affection for one another, but Edna resists me and leaves because I killed my best friend out of jealousy and rage in a duel. My favorite line in the story as I am trying to explain to Edna what happened with the duel, '*While I stood there, I was transformed; the soul of St. Elmo seemed to pass away—a fiend took possession of me; love died, hope with it—and an insatiable thirst for vengeance set my blood on fire.*'"

"Oh, well done, Cliff. I love this story," Olive blurted out. Cliff nodded.

"Now *Kathleen Mavourneen* is actually an Irish song and means '*My Beloved.*' In the play, Kathleen, played by Eunice, is a sweet, young Irish girl engaged to be married to me, Terrence Moore. Kathleen is kidnapped by an evil squire who forces her into marriage. Terrence is the hero. But I am not going to say how it ends."

"Do you know all of those parts on top of the ones you are currently doing?" I asked in astonishment.

"About as well as I know any. I'll have to brush up of course," Cliff replied matter-of-factly.

"Brush up, hell," Vic said. "The guy has a photographic memory. I can hand him a script and the next day he knows it. Comes in real handy when we need an understudy."

Cliff rolled his eyes. "Give me a break," he said.

"When do you get a break?" Olive asked.

"Yeah, when do I get a break?" Cliff said to Vic.

"How about Tuesday from three to four pm?" Vic replied.

"I'll believe that when I see it," Cliff snarled under his breath with a glint in his eye.

"You amaze me," I said to Cliff.

"That is certainly my intention." He winked.

It occurred to me at that moment just how short our time together was going to be.

35

A true friend stabs you in the front.

~OSCAR WILDE (1854–1900)

As Cliff later told me, it all happened when Cliff and Vic were alone in the office. They were both apparently in a foul mood.

"Cliff, there is something I need to say." Vic was chewing on a piece of straw.

"Go ahead."

"About Adella, you are not really considering taking her with you? Right?"

"Why do you say that?"

"She's too young for you, never been anywhere, she's way too impressionable, and she'll never stay with you. What is she seventeen or eighteen?"

"I don't see it that way, Vic."

"You don't want to see it that way. Cliff, you know I love you like a brother. I just don't see how you can do this to that innocent little girl. If you truly love her, you need to think about what this life on the road following you around would do to her. You need to think about her, not about what you want. I know. I've done what you want to do. The only difference is that Eunice already was in our world. Adella is very far from it."

"What if you're wrong? What if this is what she really wants, and what if she fits right in? She is a performer. Her music, it defines her life."

"Yeah, and you're going take that away from her? You're a fool, Cliff. She won't go back to school. She won't have her job. She won't be in one place long enough to establish herself as a musician. It will destroy all you love about her."

"That's not all I love about her…So are you suggesting that I just leave her here and never see her again? That I forget all that she means to me? All because we might have a few rough years on the road? Jesus Christ, Vic. I cannot do that. I would give up this job before I did that."

"Oh, so now what you do is just a job that you can throw away? You're even a bigger fool than I thought."

"I've already given up my bloody name. I'll be dammed if I give her up, too."

"You never wanted that name anyway."

"Your concern may not matter anyway." Cliff rubbed his hands through his hair.

"What do you mean?"

"She has not decided to come with me." They were both silent.

"Maybe you need to talk to her. Tell her that it's not the right time. Tell her to go back to school in Kansas City, finish her schooling, and maybe after a few years it will make more sense for you to be together."

Cliff put his head in his hands. "I don't think so," Cliff said under his breath so Vic could not hear.

36

ISHMAEL
~ MRS. E.D.N. SOUTHWORTH (1819–1899)

*By a woman came sin and death into the world, and by a
woman came redemption and salvation. Oh, Claudia, my Eve,
farewell! farewell! And Bee, my Mary, hail!*

The first four shows of the season went well. Cliff was right though; we
did not have a chance to spend much time with each other. On the
Monday after the fourth show, Cliff surprised me with tickets to see the
opera, *Don Quichotte*, at the Shubert. He and I had special box seats with
Vic, Eunice, and the ladies from the company. The opera was very well
done for a road show. Afterward, Cliff took me right home. He was quiet
and distant. He gave me a kiss on my forehead when he said good night.
Something was not right.

Practice for *Ishmael* started the next day. Cliff did not ask me to help
him with his lines this time. At first I figured it was because he knew the
show well, having performed it at the American Theater in New York.
This was a popular show, and word was getting out that the company was
going to perform it. People were beginning to purchase their tickets early.
The paper published an article, which read:

The beautiful old fashioned drama of the south dramatized from Mrs. E.D.N. Southworth's famous novel, 'Ishmael' or 'Risen from The Depths' will be given by the Van Dyke and Eaton Company all this week. Millions have read the novel, and those who have done so will find that the play will reawaken the interest in life that the novel no doubt did when read. It is a play which holds all that is essential to the making of a good one. Mr. Hastings will have a chance to distinguish himself in the title role, and Miss Bessie Jackson will show to advantage in the role of the imperious southern beauty. Mr. Brandon will be cast in the role of the loveable old judge and benefactor of 'Ishmael' and Miss Darette will be his friend and helpmate.

For this play, Cliff was not going to do specialties, so I had no opportunity to be alone with him during the day. McCoy and Foster were set to do the specialties. McCoy's magic act did not involve singing, but Foster's did have a few songs. The only accompaniment the company needed from me was during Foster's act and to just play select music during the scene changes. Oftentimes, Cliff went off somewhere with Bessie to work. She seemed to me to be quite demanding of his time and attention.

I have no doubt that he was feeling a little more pressure from this role, so I did not feel it was my place to ask him how it all was going. I could not let this lapse in attention from him divert me. I had to stay focused. But I couldn't help feel left out. It began to occur to me that maybe he was changing his mind about his feelings. There were no more roses at my piano bench or quaint little love notes. He just poured himself into his work and had no intention of letting me into his world.

I was usually released from the rehearsal before the cast, and Cliff went back to having a stagehand see me safely home. This was becoming rather difficult for me. I must say though, Cliff was never ungentlemanly. But I certainly perceived a distance that had not been there before.

Ishmael opened on Thursday. The company gave another performance on Friday and two performances on Saturday. The Sunday news review read:

The popularity of the Van Dyke and Eaton company was even more firmly established by their beautiful production of the play of temperament, Ishmael, which was presented to two crowded houses yesterday. The play was beautifully mounted from the scenic standpoint as well as the costuming and was admirably acted from all standpoints. In the character of Ishmael, Mr. Hastings has done the best work so far on the season bringing to the character the impetuosity of youth, and the fire and genius necessary for the role. Mr. Foster as the old overseer, who appeared just as young as he used to be, was well-received, as was Alice Jackson, the aunt of Ishmael, and who late in life tried to atone for her late marriage to society. Bessie Jackson as the haughty beauty, who valued rank and wealth above a true affection, gave a very likeable performance of a very unlikable character, while Miss Darette as the staunch hearted friend won many new admirers. Mr. Baker gave a clean cut performance of the father of Ishmael and Mr. Brandon was good as the old Judge. Mr. McCoy as the English lord did little, but as usual did it well, making up in his specialty for lack of work in the drama. Mr. Smith made a manly looking captain Burghe. The illustrated songs by Mr. Foster and the traveloque feature both were extremely entertaining and pleasing.

37

When the gods wish to punish us, they answer our prayers.
~OSCAR WILDE (1854–1900)

On Sunday, I went to church and sang in the choir. I was alone, and Cliff had not mentioned spending time with me on this day even though he technically had the day off. I was sure that he was already working on the next show, *The Embezzler,* where he played the district attorney. This show was going to be performed Tuesday, Wednesday, Thursday, Friday and Saturday night. On Saturday during the day, they would be in rehearsals for the next play, which started on Sunday. McCoy was going to be doing the specialties for this show as well, and no special songs were planned. At the Wednesday night show, the company would hand out free gifts. Tuesday night was ladies free night. Souvenir photos with Cliff and other cast members would be taken on Thursday night.

After church, I wanted to go somewhere to play the piano, just not any-where near the Club Theater. I was not sure I wanted to see him, because I was hurting and not real sure what was happening to us. The piano at the church was available, so I spent about three hours working on some new music. The time flew by, and before I knew it, it was after three o'clock. When I arrived at home, Papa was at the saloon, and Mama was busy doing chores.

"Have you heard anything from Cliff?" I asked Mama.

"No, but I haven't been home all day."

"I haven't seen much of him these past several days."

"Well, he's probably pretty busy and downright exhausted."

On Monday, I was scheduled to be at the theater at nine in the morning for an all-day rehearsal. When I arrived, the theater was dark and appeared empty. I figured that I would do my work and then go right home at the appropriate hour. Vic was the first to arrive after me.

"Have you seen Cliff?" Vic asked as he gave me a friendly hug.

"No, not for a few days," I said. Vic ignored that comment.

"I thought he would be here by now," Vic said, looking around the auditorium.

"Was he at home when you left?"

"I never thought to check on him," Vic said. He started to walk away and then turned. "Here's the music that you need to play for this one. There is nothing special here. Just play like you have during the scene changes, and we'll see how it goes." He handed me a notebook of music.

Soon, Bessie Jackson and Alice Jackson arrived along with Miss Darette, Mr. Foster, and McCoy. They were followed by Mr. Baker, Mr. Smith, and Mr. Brandon. The men moved chairs to form on circle on the stage. Cliff came running from the front of the theater and came right over to the piano. He put his arms around me from the back. I did not look at him.

"Della, I want to talk to you later," he said out of breath as if he'd been running for miles. "Do not leave without seeing me," he whispered. Then he bounded for the stage with his playbook in hand.

Now, I really did not know what to expect. What if I wanted to leave without seeing him? What if I just did not want to deal with this? If he wanted to end our friendship, I did not want to do it in person. A simple note would work. I could feel my temper flare; I wanted to scream. Not the most professional feeling that I have ever had.

The run-through of this play was more difficult than any I had seen. Cliff was short with his fellow actors at times and they with him. He was in an ugly mood, which was not characteristic of him, ever. They decided to break up at five and reconvene the rehearsal at ten in the morning for one full dress rehearsal, followed by the show at seven. Before I could get my music packed up and out of there, he was by my side.

"I need to talk to you. Can we go somewhere?"

"No, I have to be somewhere," I said.

"Della, just hear me out. Then I will take you wherever you have to be." By now everyone had left the theater.

"Talk to me here."

"I want to be alone with you. I'm not sure we're alone," he said, looking around the auditorium. He was looking to see if Jenkins was about.

"What for, Cliff?" He turned his back and walked away, and then turned abruptly back toward me.

"Because I do."

"For the past week, you've been ignoring me. I cannot go back and forth with you. Just tell me what you want and let me get on with my evening." He took my hand and pulled me over to one of the auditorium seats. He sat down beside me.

"Just hear me out. Okay? About a week ago, Vic and I were talking. He chastised me for even thinking about taking you on the road with me. He suggested that I was being a selfish fool for taking you away from your music and your schooling and the life that you know here in Joplin."

"He said that to you?"

"He's just thinking about you, Della, and he accused me of not thinking about you, which got me to thinking that I wasn't thinking about you enough and that I had no right to have expectations."

"What expectations?"

"That you would go on the road with me."

I had to be honest with him. I had not made the decision to go on the road with him. In fact, I was leaning more in the other direction. There had to be another way. I thought I would push him a little more.

"I have not agreed to go with you on the road."

"I know that." He put his head in his hands. We were silent for a moment before he spoke again.

"The more I thought about it, the more I got to brooding about it, and I decided to try and pull away, for your sake. But I cannot. I have been miserable. I do not want to pull away from you. Call me selfish, but don't expect me to be the gallant one here that will do what is right for you."

"Cliff, I am only eighteen years old as everyone keeps reminding me. I have little experience with this kind of thing. But I do know one thing. You do not have to make the decision of my life for me. If this is the only decision I ever make for myself, please let it be my decision. Vic, and I'm sure others, want you to treat me like I am a child incapable of making this decision. You should not have to make this decision for me. I will make the decision, and if I make the wrong decision, then I'll live with the consequences."

He spoke sternly and with conviction. "I want you to be with me, and I do not want that decision to be the wrong decision."

That was probably the most wonderful thing that he could have said to me at that moment. Here I was thinking that he was about to run off with Bessie Jackson and that he wanted to politely, and in his gentle way, let me go. I could feel my heart pound. This was one of my happiest moments.

We had dinner together and spent the evening at Cliff's house. Everyone else had gone out to the saloons to gamble, and Cliff would probably be with them if I weren't in his life. Instead, Cliff wanted to spend a quiet evening with me. I played the piano, and he read. He took me home at ten so we would both get a good night's sleep.

As it turned out, the show was a smashing hit. Cliff seemed in much better spirits since we had our talk. The headline in the news said,

THE EMBEZZLER SCORES A BIG HIT

The Embezzler as presented by the Van Dyke and Eaton company was a decided success from every standpoint. Beautifully costumed and well-acted it proved a bright spot in superior theatrical records. The various members of the company acquitted them-selves most creditably, and added new laurels to those they have already won since their advent in Joplin. Miss Jackson as the southern belle was well cast and gave a convincing rendition of her part—a veritable southern rose. Miss Darette, the lady with the hair, provides much amusement as did Mr. Foster as the old colored servant, whose lapse of memory caused so much trouble. Mr. McCoy as the young northerner, who steps into all breaches and straightens out all tangles was well-received. Messrs. Baker and Smith as the two old southern gentlemen were both good. The part of the young district attorney, taken by Clifford Hastings, was remarkably well-handled—he at all times being clean-cut and convincing. Mr. Brandon as the embezzling bank cashier gave a good portrayal of a difficult role. The part of Kate was well taken by Alice Jackson.

The specialties are becoming more and more pleasing with each performance, and are in fact, as good as any ever seen in the city at any theatre. Mr. McCoy's varied line of illusions and magical acts stamp him as a performer out of the ordinary.

38

LENA RIVERS

Based upon Mary J. Holmes most popular novel.
Play by Ned Albert
And I'll love, honor and obey you for the rest of my nach'ral days!

The company decided to produce *Lena Rivers* next, another three-act play that was well received in Joplin. Again, Cliff played Bessie Jackson's lover in this play, Durward Bellmont. I decided that my best way of coping with all of this was just to find ways for me to be there for him. I had to think of little things that I could do to make his life easier or at least, better. He had a girl at the house that cleaned for him and took care of his laundry. He wouldn't want me to do that anyway. With Mama's help, I could cook special things for him, like cookies, cakes, and pies. But I wasn't sure he would want that from me. He really didn't eat that much. Maybe I just needed to stay out of his way.

The company had now put on six plays, and *Lena Rivers* was the seventh. He had five more plays to do before the season ended. That meant I had five more weeks before I made my decision. If Cliff had his way, I would go with him, but he would not try to exert undue influence on me. I think he understood that it was my decision and mine only.

Cliff was not doing the specialties this time; rather McCoy was continuing to do his magic acts. As Cliff was looking over my music for this show, I thought I would ask him about the specialties.

"Cliff, are you not interested in doing the specialties?"

"Della, I just decided to take a break. Let McCoy get some glory for a while. It'll do him good." He sat next to me at the piano. "You know, I do miss performing with you, though."

"What do you think it would be like if I was on the road with you?"

"Pretty damn wonderful." He smiled.

"Do you see me performing with you on the stage?"

"I do."

"What about music?"

"Wherever the opportunity arises, I would support your decision to perform your music."

"Will there be an opportunity for that?"

"Most theaters have their own piano players. But if we did Vaudeville between acts, I don't see why I couldn't have you play the piano for me."

"Do you think I could get parts in any of the plays?"

"That would be real nice if you could, and we would certainly give it a try. You read superbly, Della. Getting you a part would only be a matter of theatrical politics. It would be gradual for that reason alone. No one would want to give you a part right away for fear that the rest of the cast would be put out by it."

"People are that way, aren't they?"

"Especially performers."

It was quiet for a minute. "You know," he said. "I am somewhat relieved that you are asking me these questions. They are good questions, and you certainly deserve to know what I think. It also tells me that you are thinking about this very seriously."

You have no idea, I thought.

"Cliff? How can I help you with this next play?"

"Let's go to my house. We'll work on my lines."

We stood and left the theater together. He took my hand as we walked along the road to his house. The house was dark when we got there, and no one appeared to be home.

"Where is everyone?" I said.

"I think some of them either went to dinner or to the saloon."

We went into the house, and Cliff led me back to the kitchen.

"There's got to be something to eat in the icebox," he said.

Before he turned on the light in the kitchen, he turned and wrapped his arms around me. It was still dark. His mouth found mine and kissed me like he hadn't kissed me in a while. I wound my hands around his neck, and we stood there in the dark in a deep kiss for the longest time. I never wanted this to end. While we were kissing, he unbuttoned my coat and let it fall to the floor. I fell back against the wall in the hallway. He did not back away. He reached around behind me, grabbed me at the small of my back, and pulled me against him. I could hear his breath quicken.

"Della, I want to take you upstairs," he whispered in my hair.

"Okay," I said as his mouth crushed into mine. I had no idea what would happen if I went upstairs with him, but I felt like I was on fire.

Then we both heard someone opening the door.

"Come on." He pulled me by the hand into the kitchen and sat me at the table. He switched the light on by the table and poured us both a brandy as Vic and Eunice arrived home.

"I'm not sure whether to curse them or thank them," he said, winking at me.

My coat was still on the floor in the hallway, and my hair was a mess. We both were chuckling to ourselves as Vic and Eunice came into the kitchen. Vic had my coat in his hand.

"Drop something?" he said with a smirk on his face.

"Actually I did," Cliff said. "I had trouble finding the light."

"I bet that wasn't all you had trouble with," Vic said as he smiled at me. He poured himself a brandy and sat down next to me at the table. "How are you, Adella?"

Eunice poured herself a glass of wine and sat down on the other side of me.

"Vic, I've never been better, really. The fact that I might give up my music and my schooling and follow you and Cliff around the country has me so depressed I could slit my wrists."

Eunice gasped and then chuckled.

"I guess I deserve that," Vic said.

"Yes, you do," Eunice chimed in.

Cliff just sat there and looked wonderfully amused at my sarcasm.

Before I knew it, the play had its first two runs. Joplin loved *Lena Rivers,* and that love brought in large crowds. The reviewer said:

Probably the most pronounced hit of anything yet produced by the Van Dyke and Eaton company at the Club was the production of 'Lena Rivers' at the matinee and night performances yesterday. Large crowds witnessed both performances and were unanimous in their praise of play and players. Of dramatized novels, it probably follows the story more closely than any, and thereby gives the satisfaction as a drama that it did as a book.

Miss Bessie Jackson, who in the beginning is an unsophisticated foundling, brings a natural grace and sweetness to the role. Her development throughout the various acts is natural. Miss Darette as the spoiled child was an excellent foil, and played a trying part most admirably, while Alice Jackson was pleasing as the quaint old Granny Nichols and sufficiently detestable as the second Mrs. Graham.

Mr. McCoy as the country yokel, who develops a remarkable shrewd mind, was satisfactory, as were also his illusions and magic specialties between acts. Mr. Hastings was an acceptable lover, and Mr. Foster as the tried parent of a spoiled child was good as always. Mr. Brandon, as Lena's father, and Mr. Baker as the oldest inhabitant had little to do but did that little well. The whole show was given with a finish and exactness that showed careful study and painstaking attention to detail. The play will finish out the week with the usual bargain matinee on Saturday.

This really was Bessie Jackson's show, because she delighted the audience as the adorable Miss Lena Rivers. The white performers played the colored parts in this show, Aunt Milly and Old Caesar, and kept the audience laughing. Neither McCoy nor Cliff was particularly fond of this review. It did not help that everyone in the company started calling Cliff "the acceptable lover" and McCoy "the country yokel."

39

OUT OF THE FOLD

BY LANGDON MCCORMICK

*'Out of the Fold' is what is commonly termed a pastoral
play, and the theme is as pure and sweet as a spring
of snow water, and grips the interest of the auditor from the
beginning to the end.*

~UNKNOWN

Before *Lena Rivers* had finished, Cliff began work on his next play, a sad story that turned positive in the end. He felt it would be a breath of fresh air to lighten up the mood amongst the company players. The article in Monday's newspaper reported:

> *'Out of the Fold', a pastoral play taken from the parable of the lost sheep is the production to be staged by the Van Dyke and Eaton company this week. The play is not dissimilar in plot to 'Way Down East', a wayward college student, a deceived girl, and a host of rural characters all involved in a mix-up that comes out right in the end, turning what threatens to be a tragedy into a first class comedy.*

Cliff played the schoolmaster, while McCoy was the villainous rival for the affection of Helene, who, of course, was played by none other than Miss Bessie Jackson. But something wonderful happened during this play. McCoy and Bessie developed a chemistry both on and off stage. At first, Cliff did not believe me when I mentioned to him that I thought there was something more going on between them. Then he started noticing the same things I saw.

Eunice brought it up during dinner at the house.

"I've noticed another romance budding in the company," she said.

"If it is true, it'll be good for both of them," Cliff added.

"By the way Mick talks, they might get married and soon," Vic said.

"Really?" I said.

"I guess Mick would move out of here and in with Bessie at the other house," Eunice said.

"Cliff, what would you think if they got married as a specialty during one of the plays?" Vic said.

"I've seen it done before. In fact, I was in one play where we had a marriage during one intermission, and Judge Karol, the Democratic candidate for the governor of Wisconsin, spoke during another intermission because he was up for reelection. Neither event scared the audience away. But since I theoretically end up as Bessie's lover in this play, it might be a bit odd to have her marry McCoy during a scene change."

We all laughed at the image this created in our minds.

"If they do get married," I said, "we will need to have a party for them, and I will gladly help with planning that party."

"You may not have much time to plan, because I'm thinking this wedding could happen faster than a shotgun wedding." Vic smirked.

The play went well despite the relationship between McCoy and Bessie. The crowds were ready for a comedy. Cliff and others performed Vaudeville between the acts and received a raving review, *The olios are exceptionally good and helped materially in the long waits between acts.* The news article gave it a pretty good review, as each play was described as more popular than the last.

The present play at the Club is without a doubt the most popular one that has been presented at this theatre by the Van Dyke and Eaton company. Differing in every way from all of the others it came as a pleasant surprise, and more than pleased two capacity houses at the matinee and night performances yesterday. 'Out of the Fold' is what is commonly termed a pastoral play, and the theme is as pure and sweet as a spring of snow water, and grips the interest of the auditor from the beginning to the end.

The different members of the company acquitted themselves most admirably. Miss Bessie Jackson as the erring school mistress handling a delicate role in a most pleasing manner, with her natural simplicity, and yet bringing to her stronger scenes a flood of emotion that went straight to the heart. Mr. Hastings, as the schoolmaster and in love with his assistant was manly and gave a true rendition of a manly role. Mr. Baker as the college friend who has seen the world was good, and Mr. McCoy as the precocious boy was at his best. Mr. Foster had two characters, that of the town bully and the genial old judge, and both were well done.

On the last night of this play, at the very end, Jimmy McCoy and Bessie Jackson were married on the stage for all of their fans to see. We had a party for them in the foyer area of the theater with cake, coffee, or tea. There was a beautiful three-tier cake made by one of the women from my church with a bride and groom and small red roses made of frosting across the top. Some of the girls from my church charity group helped serve the cake and beverages. Both Jimmy and Bessie were appreciative of the work that I had done to put this reception together for them on such short notice. After the reception, all of the members of the company and I went down to the Criterion saloon to celebrate. There were a lot of jokes about Jimmy being a "country yokel" and Cliff being "manly" as the paper had described. As Eunice predicted, Jimmy did move into Bessie's house that night.

Later, as we walked through town, Cliff was very quiet. He took hold of my hand.

"What are you thinking?" I asked.

"Just thinking about what a good day this has been."

"You seemed quieter than usual tonight. I guess I am used to you being more animated than you were."

"I'm just real happy for them. And I couldn't help but think that maybe that would be you and I someday."

I said nothing more to him about the "you and I" comment. I understood how he could feel that way, but I knew that it would never be that way for Cliff and me. We were different in many ways from Jimmy and Bessie. For one, they had lived the same kind of life and had a much better chance of making their relationship work than Cliff and I ever would have.

40

THE LITTLE MINISTER
BY JAMES M. BARRIE

*The life of every man is a diary in which he means to write
one story and writes another; and his humblest hour is when he
compares the volume as it is with what he vowed to make it.*

The company management made a last-minute change in the play to be
done the next week. Instead of doing *In Panama* as was planned, they
decided to produce *The Little Minister* with Cliff playing the part of Rob
Dow, McCoy as Gavin Dishart, the minister, and Bessie Jackson as Babbie,
the aristocrat disguised as a gypsy to avoid a predetermined marriage to
someone she did not love. The play was set in Scotland. Cliff played a
drunken weaver in this play and, like Vic, also had a knack for portraying
a drunk.

This switch sent the company into frenzy because it was so last minute.
Apparently, there were patrons of the theater who wanted to see this play
done because it had been made into a silent film in 1913.

Cliff told me that this play was also based upon the popular novel by
James M. Barrie, who was best known for his 1904 novel and play, *Peter*

Pan. Cliff also informed me that his character dies in this play trying to save Dishart, the minister, and Rintoul, the nobleman that Babbie was supposed to marry. What neither of us knew at the time was that this play would be made into a talking movie in 1934 with Katherine Hepburn as Babbie.

On Saturday night, after the finish of *Out of the Fold*, Cliff took me home so he could start working on his lines for *The Little Minister*. It had been some time since he had performed this play, and he didn't think he had the lines down as well as some of the others. Although Sunday was his day off, the company decided to have a read-through in the afternoon.

Cliff arrived at nine thirty to take me to church.

"You should be home memorizing your lines," I said to him as he came up the stairs to our home.

"There's plenty of time for that," he said. "I want to go to church with you. After church, I have rehearsal all afternoon. Then, I am going to ask you for a favor of running lines with me, tonight, at my house. We'll have dinner. Are you free to spend the evening with me?"

"Sure I am. But do you think you will have a moment's peace at church?"

"I'll sit in the back."

I think Cliff was bound and determined to show me that our relationship could work, that he was willing to come into my world as much as his schedule would allow. I must say that it felt good to have him with me.

He came to the saloon after the rehearsal. Mama had prepared Sunday dinner for us, surprising Cliff because he loved Mama's cooking.

After dinner, we walked to his house and began working on his lines in the sitting room. This play called for a Scottish dialect, and he was wonderful at it.

The opening night went very well. I played piano during the scene changes, and even my piano selections had a Scottish flavor. The newspaper article was appreciative of Cliff's work:

Prettiest Play Yet

The Little Minister last night was a beautiful production of a beautiful story. The play was exceptionally well-received by the audience. The play is effectively staged and costumed. The opening scene shows the mountains

> *beyond the town in the foreground with the town in the distance reddening through night air, a beautiful scene, most effectively arranged, and the staging of the whole production is in keeping.*
>
> *Scotch dialect, Scotch mannerism and Scotch humor is well maintained throughout the play. Tammas and the other two pillars of the kirk 'in their blacks' introduce a delicious comedy and the reading of the minister's love poem is one of the particular happy things of the play. 'Her boy am I' is today a byword of fun and laughter in Joplin.*
>
> *No better acting has been seen in Joplin than Cliff Hastings as Rob Dow. Mr. Hasting's conception of this difficult part is one of the very best things of a production full of good things.*
>
> *One of the most pleasing portions of the play is the clever scene when Nannie and Babbie give the Little Minister a dish of tea.*

On the last night of this play, Cliff and I left the theater together. The plan was to meet up with the rest of the cast at Bessie's house for a nightcap. It was a cool night. As we walked, Cliff took my hand as he usually did.

"You know, that play reminds me of you and I," he said.

"How is that?"

"I think we have been touched by forbidden love. I should write our story in a play—it would make for a good melodrama. Beautiful and talented pianist from Joplin meets traveling actor ten years her senior. They have a torrid love affair for a few months when their worlds collide. And they just cannot seem to bring their worlds together. In the end, they part ways, and neither is better for it."

"That sounds like a terribly sad play."

"In a way, it's worse than death. These two characters have all of the opportunity to be together, but they are trapped in their own box and it's suffocating them."

"It sounds like you have no hope for us."

"Love is an irresistible desire to be irresistibly desired," Cliff said, quoting Walt Whitman.

"I think love is much more than that. Love could mean having the sense to know when to part ways."

"And that, my dear, is why my heart is heavy. I have no doubt there will come a time when you will decide to part ways."

41

MAN OF THE HOUR

BY GEORGE BROADHURST

*Because I have been quiet, it does not necessarily
mean I have been asleep.*

U ntil Cliff had talked about me letting him go, I had not really thought
about how that would feel. Now, at the start of the rehearsals for this
play, it occurred to me that the company would be in Joplin for only three
more weeks. The winter season seemed to be passing quickly. I knew what
Cliff wanted me to do, but he hadn't really pushed me to make the decision.
I expect that he wanted me to make the decision absent pressure from him to
do what he wanted, so we both avoided talking about it. I did not want him
to go, but I was not prepared for how I would feel when he was truly gone.

Jenkins had indicated to me that it was likely that the Club would
close for remodeling after this season, which meant that I would not have a
job playing the piano. Olive was still in Kansas City, and I still thought it
would be appropriate for me to go there and finish my schooling.

The last few weeks with Cliff wasn't all work though his schedule continued to be grueling. Even though his schedule was full seven days a week,
we spent a good deal of time together. A couple times when he was not

performing, he took me to an opera or musical performance at the Shubert. We took the train to Springfield for a day to shop, eat, and just walk around the town. We spent a lot of time playing cards, laughing, and singing with members of the company after the shows or rehearsals.

Cliff told me that one of his favorite theaters was the Warrington Opera House in Oak Park, Illinois. He was in a series of plays there in 1910. He told me that if he ever had the chance to settle down, it would be in Oak Park. It was a quaint village, but near enough to Chicago to get the benefits of the big city. He told me that when he left the theater, not if, but when, that he wanted to manage his own business and travel.

We spoke about traveling together to see Chicago and New York City. I told him that I would love to travel and see the world, and he talked about taking me back to Bristol, England, to meet his family. He spoke about wanting to become a citizen of the United States and that he had filed a declaration to do so.

We talked about my charity work through the church. I learned that Cliff and the whole company were charitable and interested in doing what they could to support a worthwhile cause. They often donated food, toys, and dolls to children and spent a lot of time doing free performances to raise money for the needy.

We talked about plays, music, and literature. I think Cliff had read every book and play that was written, constantly searching for new material. He liked to listen to me play anything on the piano, especially something that I had improvised. He was always ordering new sheet music for me from a music store in St. Louis.

We both read the news and talked about what was going on in our world, the war overseas and all of the changes that were taking place in our own country. Neither of us could foresee the effect that the war was going to have our lives in the next year.

Aside from the changes in the theater and motion picture industry, automobile ownership was starting to gain popularity. The telephone was being introduced into our part of the world, and we both realized how different a world it was going to be just to be able to call people when you wanted to talk to them. Clothing styles were even changing as women's hemlines and haircuts began to get shorter.

Cliff told me a little more about his family and about his father. He described how they had parted ways. Since then, his mother and his sister would write to him when he was in one place for any period of time. He spoke of his brother who lived in Boston and his uncles who worked the family iron works business in England. We spoke of England, and he described what he thought his life would have been like if he had stayed there.

He once even mentioned to me that if I went back to Kansas City, he would only be a few hours away, at least, for a while.

The Man of the Hour ran Wednesday, Thursday, Friday, and two shows on Saturday. Cliff did not do specialties for this show. In fact, no one did.

His portrayal of Alwyn Bennett was wonderful. Bessie was at her best as his true love, Dallas Wainright. Helen DeLand played Mrs. Bennett and had one of Papa's favorite lines in the play when she said, *"My husband used to say that most of the men who rise high in finance do it by mounting the corpses of those they had despoiled and betrayed."* Papa sure didn't think much of bankers, politicians, or the rich folk that they catered to. Vic played the nasty Mr. Wainright, and McCoy was his cohort, Horrigan.

There was a part in this play when I felt like Cliff was talking to me. He was really talking to Dallas, but the words had more meaning to Cliff and me. *"No matter what I do, it will mean nothing—unless you share it. I have grown since you went away. As I have grown, my love for you has grown. It is the one thing in my life—the one thing in my life—the one real thing—success, power, office will mean nothing without you."*

The Joplin newspaper review was very good.

VAN DYKE-EATON TROUPE DRAWS CROWDED HOUSES AT THEATRE

'The Man of the Hour' Proves to be a Successful Play

Two capacity houses welcomed the Van Dyke and Eaton Company. The play for the engagement was George Broadhurst's most successful play, 'The Man of the Hour,' and at the hands of this capable company left little, if anything, to be desired, and surely nothing when the prices are taken into consideration. The company was admirably suited to the portrayel of the drama, and each and every one gave a good account of themselves in their respective roles. Mr. Hastings as the trifling society man, without an aim in life, and suddenly thrust into politics at the hands of an unscrupulous 'boss,' had the best part he has had bringing a young manliness and sturdy sense of right and wrong to his work that appealed to all and won him much admiration and commendation.

42

St. Elmo
~By Augusta J. Evans

Man-like is it to fall into sin,
Fiend-like is it to dwell therein,
Christ-like is it for sin to grieve,
God-like is it all sin to leave.

The rehearsal for *St Elmo* was intense and more emotionally draining because Cliff played a man fraught with jealousy and rage. This show was scheduled to begin immediately after *The Man of the Hour* with two shows on Sunday. So the company began rehearsals for *St. Elmo* while they were performing the other play. There was a lot of set work to be done on this play, so when he wasn't rehearsing, Cliff was tied up "assisting" the set crew with the final preparations. McCoy was back to doing his magic specialty.

After opening night, the news article about St. Elmo read:

ST. ELMO' TOMORROW NIGHT

The Van Dyke and Eaton Company scored one of the biggest hits of the season with their beautiful production of the famous play, 'St. Elmo,' which was presented to two capacity houses Sunday matinee and night. The play has all of the elements of a great one and there was nothing left undone by the different members of the cast or the management to make this a noteworthy production in every sense of the word. The acting was characterized by a quiet intenseness that carried conviction with it, and while it is entitled to the title of intellectual, there was at no time a sense of dullness or dragging so common to a quiet play.

Miss Jackson as the orphan Edna gave a comprehensive and painstaking performance of a most difficult role and more than ever convinced her audience that she is a little woman of exceptional ability and remarkable talent. Miss Darette and Alice Jackson gave creditable performances of uncongenial roles. Mr. Hastings, in the name part 'St Elmo' gave a splendid performance of the wild and tempestuous boy whose life had been blighted through ill-treatment at the hands of friends, and showed a remarkable, keen perception of his character in the latter stages when the all-powerful influence of a great spirit possessed him. Mr. Brandon was well-received as the minister, and gave a clean cut performance of a most lovable character, while Mr. Baker in the dual role of the erring son and the bibulous doctor, was at his best. Mr. Foster also handled a dual role of the old blacksmith and the young rake and did both admirably. Mr. McCoy was alone in his glory and furnished the amusement of the evening in the character of the young inventor. The new specialties were entertaining and instructive. The play will not be given tonight on account of the big road attraction, "Ready Money" which appears at the Grand this evening.

St. Elmo will be given on Tuesday, Wednesday and Thursday nights.

On Wednesday night after the play, Cliff and I went back to his house. Eunice and Vic met us there, along with Will Foster, Orrin Burke, Jimmy and Bessie McCoy, Alice Jackson, Miss Darette, and Mr. Brandon. It was a party in a sense, but they all kept running their lines together and arguing about various scenes and parts of the play. Everyone was drinking wine. Eunice pulled me back into the kitchen.

"Adella, I hate to ask you this, but I am dying to know—what are you going to do?"

"You really do not want to know my answer."

"Why is that?"

"Because I don't have one. I have not decided to go anywhere, just yet."

"Time is ticking, sweetie." She looked at me, smiled, and touched my arm. "I really would not want to be in your position. I know this must be hard for you. But he is scheduled to leave here on a train the day after the last show. That is exactly fourteen days from now. He has business to take care of up in St. Joseph, and I know he has been working hard to see if he can find a suitable place for us to live."

"He doesn't talk about leaving to me. I don't think he wants to pressure me into making a decision."

"That's Cliff...always the gentleman." She was quiet for a few moments as we prepared plates of finger food to take out to the starving guests.

"Are you all leaving at the same time?"

"Yes, I think so. Some may be on a later train than others. I'm not quite sure." We could hear Vic calling Eunice from the other room.

"I must go wait on my liege," she said with a smirk. Leave it to Eunice to be sarcastic. As she was leaving, Cliff walked in.

"Get out of my way, squire," she said to him as he took some food off her plate and put it in his mouth.

"Yes, your highness," he jokingly bowed to her. "Have you been in here torturing my lady?" he said in the perfect English accent.

"No more than you torture her every day."

He arched his brow, and Eunice theatrically disappeared down the hallway.

Cliff moved over to me, gently turned me to face him, and wrapped me up in his embrace. He put his forehead to mine.

"How are you?"

"Tired, but I'm glad to be here with you, if that's what you mean."

"Well, I'm going to take you home and then turn in myself. We have a helluva day tomorrow."

"I am forever amazed at how you do this. Will you have a break before the season starts in St. Joseph?"

"Yes, I think about a week this time," he said quietly.

Our eyes met. He looked sad. I think he could sense what my answer was going to be.

"I don't think I'm ready to go on the road."

"I don't want to leave you here. I want you with me."

He started pacing.

"What if I gave all of this up and stayed here with you? I could do that."

He stopped pacing and looked at me. At first, I couldn't tell if he was practicing a line from the play or being real.

"I would never let you do that."

Tears formed in my eyes, so I looked away. I knew that having him give up what he loved to do for me would surely be the end of us. I loved him too much to ever let that happen.

"So," he said, "it's not okay for me to decide it's not in your best interest to go on the road with me, but it is okay for you to decide that I should not stay here with you?" He smiled his serious smile. Our eyes met again.

"Here we are trapped in your melodrama." A tear rolled down my face.

"It'll be all right." He took me in his arms again. I lay my head against his shoulder. "If we're so brilliant at what we do, we should be able to figure this one out. Right?" he said.

"Cliff, I do love you."

He buried his face in my hair and tightened his hold on me. "No matter what you decide, I will always love you."

We must have stood there like that in the middle of the kitchen for an hour it seemed. Both of us knew what was coming, and neither of us wanted to make the first move.

43

KATHLEEN MAVOURNEEN
Based upon an Irish folk song by
Frederick William Nicholls Crouch

O hast thou forgotten how soon we must sever?
O hast thou forgotten this day we must part?
It may be for years, and it may be forever
Oh, why art thou silent, thou voice of my heart?
It may be for years, and it may be forever
Then why art thou silent, Kathleen Mavourneen?

The time for the last play of the winter season had finally arrived. The company began rehearsing this play on Friday. The play was scheduled for two performances on Sunday, one on Monday and Tuesday, with the last performance on Wednesday. Cliff would be on his way to St. Joseph on Thursday. The crew was already busy getting the sets organized for transport, the costumes packed away in traveling trunks, and the props and furnishings properly stored. All of this would be moved to railroad cars on Wednesday night after the last show.

Cliff was the lover boy hero in this show with Eunice. I was actually really looking forward to her performance. It had been quite a while since she was cast in a main role. Lorene Tolsen actually had the leading role. Vic, Mr. Brandon, and Mr. Foster were in this play, too. The stage manager, Bill Friese, was in a tizzy half of the time trying to put this last show together.

The performances went well until the last night when all hell broke loose in the theater. It was probably a tradition for the company to completely turn their last show of the season into a slapstick farce, but I was taken off guard by what happened that night.

The news described it the best:

THE STAGE HANDS QUEERED THE SHOW

Farewell performance of Stock Company at Local Theatre-Funny for the Audience

The matinee idol has feet of clay and the only true God of the stage is the lowly 'grip.' Without his favor, no person or play can get by. If this aphorism does not appeal to you as true, ask someone of the hundreds who packed the Club Theatre Wednesday night, when the VanDyke and Eaton Company closed their season. The play was 'Kathleen Mavourneen,' a mellerdrammer of the mellerest, but the hills were lost in trills of laughter, deepened into roars and rose into shrieks—when the stage hands got into their stride and began to run things. From the point in the first act where they supplied Miss Lorene Tolsen with a jug of water she could scarcely lift, instead of the tiny jug called for by the property plot, until Miss Tolsen made a farewell speech from the arms of stage manager, Mr. Bill Friese, after he had dragged the shrinking heroine before the shrieking audience, the show was a farce.

The Dancing Flowers

In the second act, Mr. Foster and Miss Elliott were having a thrilling scene, and were much disturbed when instead of sitting breathless the audience shrieked with laughter. They did not know that the flowers from a vase at the back wall of the scene were doing mad aerial dances at the end of strings let down from the flies. They 'woke up' however when an alarm clock went off with a bang just at the crisis of the scene.

There was a dark scene in the third act, and Messrs Vickery and Brandon were, to say the least, started when a white handkerchief on a rubber band zipped across the stage from side to side with nervous rapidity. In the last act the lid came off entirely. Cliff Hastings, as the hero, started in to chop down a wall to get at the villains or something, and just as he raised his trusty sledge high for the first resounding blow, the whole works fell with a crash. The stage force pulled the string, and rose triumphantly from the ruins. Somewhat flustered, Mr. Hastings started in to throw the villains off the cliff. In marched solemnly four stage hands. They seized the villains, the hero and the heroine and hustled them about the stage. Then standing upon the verge of the precipice, they solemnly waived adieu, and one by one, hurled themselves over the brink. Heaving a sign of relief as their hurdling bodies vanished, Mr. Hastings got to work and disposed of the three villains in a workmanlike manner—and in lockstepped the stage hands who had so recently hurled themselves over the precipice, picked up the protesting corpses and dragged them out.

Newspaper Storm

The grand finale came when Miss Tolsen, the leading lady, woke from her dream in the final scene. She woke, *stretched, yawned-and blam-one thousand newspapers from the flies in a blob fell, and covered up her blonde beauty. By the time she had been excavated, Bill Friese was there, and Bill grasped her by the arm and led her before the shouting audience, where she made a farewell speech.*

The theater was packed on that last night. In fact, people had to be turned away. At the end of a long season, it was traditional for each member of the company to make a speech, and as each of them appeared, they were greeted by applause. Cliff, Bessie, Vic, Foster, and McCoy were all greeted by standing ovations from the audience.

Once the show was over, the stage hands immediately started striking the set. Several of the male actors, including Cliff, helped for a while. It would be a long night for them. I wanted to ask Cliff what the hell happened to the show. Did he know about all of this fooling around? Was this something that they had planned?

Albert happened to be at this last show. He was alone. He came up behind me while I was still at the piano getting my music organized.

"Can we go somewhere and talk?" he said quietly as he touched my arm.

"Oh, Albert. How are you?" I looked around to see if Cliff was watching me. He was nowhere in sight. "I'm sorry. I have plans, Albert. Why are you here?"

"Well, we never got around to getting together like we said we were going to do."

"Yes. I know."

"Adella, are you running off with one of them?" He had a pained expression on his face.

"Albert, I do not owe you an explanation. You are engaged to be married. What the devil do you care?"

"I don't know. I've been asking myself the same question. I cannot stop thinking about you." He looked down at his hands holding his hat.

"You cannot stop thinking about me. Are you out of your mind?"

"I have strong feelings for you. I always have. I think about what we might have had together. We go back a long time, you and I."

"Albert, we said good-bye a long time ago."

"I care about you."

"Albert…"

"I don't want you wasting your life on some no account actor. You deserve so much more. I can give you that."

"No, you cannot."

The words were no sooner out of my mouth when Cliff was at the front of the stage looking down at us.

"Is everything okay, love?"

"This is an old friend of mine. Albert. We're just talking, Cliff."

"Just talking? All right," Cliff said suspiciously. He stood there looking down at the two of us. I pretended to be busy with my music.

"Albert, this is Cliff Hastings."

"I know who he is, Adella," Albert said.

"Della, I have a few more things to do. I'll give you and Albert some time to talk." Cliff walked away.

"Damn, Della, you're with him now?"

"How dare you be so critical? He is the best man I know."

"So it's all true?"

"Like I said, I do not owe you an explanation. You think what you want to think."

"Well, when you figure out what the hell you're doing for the rest of your life…if you want to talk, you know where to find me. Just remember what I said."

He leaned over and kissed me on the forehead. Then he whispered, "At least you picked the most famous one." I could see Cliff watching us. He had the strangest look on his face. Albert turned, tipped his hat at Cliff, and walked out of the theater.

I sat down on the piano bench. I was having a hard enough time dealing with all of this, and did not need to feel pressure from Albert.

I noticed Cliff and Vic talking, and then he was at my side.

"I'm all yours for as long as you like," he said, grinning. "You have no idea how good it feels to be done for a whole week. I really need the break."

"I am glad that you feel good. This is very sad for me."

He took my hand.

"It'll be all right. Let's go somewhere. Do you want to go have a drink? Some of the others might be heading to the Criterion."

"Don't they need you here to help?"

"Nope, I have completed my projects. The rest is up to them."

"Is that how we should spend our last few hours, in a saloon?"

"Oh, Della, I'm not going to look at this as our last few hours. I cannot. We are going to enjoy our night, and we'll kiss and say good night just like any other. In the morning, I'm going to take a train trip, sort of a scouting mission. It will probably be a while before I see you again, but we can write. I'll write you a letter every day, and you better write me back."

"This is not making me feel better."

His eyes met mine.

"You always have other options."

"Other options? Right."

He grabbed my hand and pulled me out a back door of the theater where we stood and talked over a year and a half ago.

"It's quieter out here," he said. "I need to think straight for a few minutes."

It was quiet again.

"What are you cooking up in your head?" I asked. He was pacing.

"Who was that guy?"

"Albert."

"I know his name. What is he to you? Do I have to be worried?"

"He's nobody."

"Sure? I'm not daft, Della."

"I have never been surer."

"You know, I have not been silent about how I feel about you and what I want to happen here. Right? You know I want us to be married as soon as possible, right?" He stepped away and ran his hands through his hair. "Geez...I feel like we've had this talk a dozen times." The frustration exuded from him.

"We have."

He was quiet again.

"I just want to make sure you understand me." He wrapped his arms around me at the small of my back.

"I think...I do."

"Good. Because when I walk away from you later tonight, it will be the hardest thing I have had to do in a long while. But I'm going do it because you want it this way, and because maybe this is just something you and I have to experience so we better understand this journey we are on together. But this is not the end for me, Della." He lifted my chin to gently kiss me.

"We're going to say good-bye tonight? Don't you want me to go with you to the station?"

"No. If you go with me to the station, I will not get on that train. I do not want you to come to the station. And Della?"

He paused, but he looked into my eyes.

"I love you so very much, and you will be with me wherever I go. Remember that."

44

Trains to nowhere will take you anywhere you want to go.
~CLIFFORD HASTINGS

We were together after Wednesday night's play until near four in the morning. Cliff was leaving around one o'clock Thursday after all of the company property was safely packed away on the train. I said my good-byes to the other members of the company. He walked me home, and we sat on the porch stoop for a while. We promised to see each other again. We kissed, and then he was gone. The pain of that experience made me numb. Something about this night felt surreal. It had to be a dream I kept thinking as I tried to fall asleep.

What was wrong with me? How could I allow this person to walk out of my life like this? Why didn't I go with him? Was he right? Was this something he and I had to experience together?

I was due back at work at the Club on Saturday night. I could not even imagine what that was going to be like. It was as if I fully expected him to still be there, along with all of the rest of the company and all their sets, costumes, furniture, and props.

I planned on spending Friday at home resting. I was not quite up to going to the theater to practice and I didn't even feel like getting dressed. For the first time in my life, Joplin felt empty. I didn't want to go anywhere that reminded me of Cliff. I tried reading for a while, but could hardly concentrate. Then I started writing Cliff a letter, one that I couldn't mail to him because I didn't have his address yet. I must have started that letter six times, and each time the paper ended up wadded in a ball in my garbage. Then I tried to play the piano, but everything that I played reminded me of Cliff.

My life here had changed because of him. I knew I would never be the same. I also knew that I was starting to have one helluva time without him here. When I wasn't crying, I was tense and mean-spirited. I tried sobbing, but that only made me feel worse. I wasn't angry at anyone but myself. Mama checked on me a few times.

"This will pass," she said.

"I doubt it, Mama."

"You knew he would be leaving here when he came last winter. I'm not sure what you expected."

"I didn't expect anything of him. He didn't let me down, Mama. I let myself down."

"What do you mean, child?"

"We do love each other, but I couldn't bring myself to fully believe in that love. I could not see myself living on the road. I was too stubborn to see myself living on the road. You know, he would have given it all up for me. I didn't even let that happen."

"That was a very good decision. Tell me, what is it that kept you from going with him?"

"You and Papa, and this home, and all of my things...my job at the Club."

"Those are not reasons to stay here if you are miserable."

"How about my fear of him, of it not working out with him, of not liking the constant pressure of being on the road and not being able to make a home with him?"

"Della, he would be your home. None of this other stuff matters one hill of beans. And what do you mean your fear of him? Has he ever done anything to make you fear him?"

"Never. But I have no idea what I am doing when it comes to being with a man. He is so worldly, and I live above a saloon in the middle of nowhere. That is what I fear."

"I have no doubt that you would come to learn all about being with a man like Mr. Hastings, given some time."

"His terms are that I would be married to him first."

"Now that's a gentleman." She paused. "You need to think long and hard about letting him go."

"I have been thinking."

"No, far as I can tell, you have been doing everything but thinkin' about it. You're eighteen, almost nineteen years old. Why a lot of girls are married by the time they are eighteen. Some even have children."

"Mama, I am in a daze. Why is everything so clear to you?"

She smiled. "You know, when he first came here, I was against this thing between you and him. I figured he was just another actor, probably with a girl in every town. That's what I thought, but he isn't that way at all. He is genuine and he is well-mannered, and I have no doubt that he truly loves you."

It was about then that Papa came upstairs. I was surprised he was home from the saloon before eight.

"What are you doing home?" Mama asked him.

I walked up to him. He had a newspaper in his hand. He would not look me in the eye as he handed me the paper.

"Take a look at this," he said.

"What is it?" I took the paper. The headline read, "Train is Wrecked." My knees buckled under me, and I slumped down in the chair.

Passenger Train Derailed Near Portage Lake While Running Thirty Miles Per Hour

The north bound M.&I. passenger due at Walker at 4:41 pm was badly wrecked near Portage Lake, about seven miles down the track. The wreck was caused by spreading of the rails and three coaches were overturned and badly demolished. Conductor Coppersmith came to Walker on the engine and securing Dr. Wilcox the railroad physician, hurried back to the scene in a boxcar.

Seven persons were found to be injured, though some of them, seriously, while all of the twenty four passengers received a good shaking up.

"Are you sure this was his train?" My hand was shaking. I could not bear it if anything happened to Cliff.

"Pretty darn sure. It was bound for Kansas City, and from there they were going on up to St. Joseph. It's been the talk of the town late this afternoon."

"How far is Walker?"

"About seventy miles."

"How long would it take me to get there?"

"Probably no trains are running on that track for a few days. They got to figure a way to get those three demolished cars off the track."

"How long would it take to go there in the car?"

"I reckon over two hours, maybe three." It was quiet. "If you don't hear from him by tomorrow morning, I'll get my friend, Murphy, to drive us up there."

Tears flooded my eyes. I had to make sure he was all right.

By morning, I had not heard from Cliff. So Papa and I headed north up Route 71 in Murphy's Model T. We left about nine and got to Walker around noon. Walker was a small town, but it probably had everything there that a town needed. The train depot looked deserted. Papa and Murphy dropped me off at the depot so I could check on the status of the trains, and they were going on up the street to have a look around the town. The inside of the depot was quiet and empty.

"Sir, could you tell me anything about the train wreck?" I asked the man behind the counter.

"Not much to tell. Most of the passengers have left. The ones with serious injuries have gone up to Kansas City to the hospital there."

"I have friends on that train. Do you have a list of the injured?"

"No, ma'am, not here, I don't."

"Are you running trains on that track yet?"

"No, they're still working on that track. Quite a mess out there. Expect it'll be a few days before they'll be running trains again."

I stared at him. He dropped his head to his work on the counter. He had no more information for me. I was devastated. Standing there in the depot, I could almost imagine that Cliff was there standing next to me. But then I thought I must be losing my mind. I was hungry, but I was also sick in my stomach. I wanted answers, but there were no answers for me here.

I stepped out onto the loading dock. It was quiet but for the wind. There were no trains running on this track. This deck area was made out of rough sawn wood. There was an old wooden bench by the depot, and I wondered if Cliff had sat on that bench. The train schedule was taped to the backside of the door but was folded over from the wind. I wondered if he had touched that schedule. I stood there in the quiet of the depot for the longest while just listening to the wind.

Maybe I should drive south to where the accident occurred. I glanced to the south, in the opposite direction of the town. Three people, men, were walking in my direction. Two of the men stopped off at a building, but the other one kept walking my way. His hands were in his coat pockets. He had a light colored straw hat and wore a long dark coat over a suit. The coat was unbuttoned in the front. The wind was blowing sand and tumbleweed in the man's direction. He looked up at me, squinting from the dust, and I could hear him yell.

"Della!"

"Cliff?" I said under my breath.

The man started running my way. I ran down the steps toward him. His forehead was bandaged, but he was safe. He grabbed me, lifted me clear off my feet, and swung me around in a circle.

"I was just going to try and contact you. What are you doing here?" He was out of breath. He kissed me and buried his face in my hair. I could feel his chest heave.

"I came to find you. Are you all right?" I touched his forehead. "You're cut."

"I am fine."

"What about the others?"

"We will all live. Some are just banged up pretty bad." He touched my face. "I cannot believe it is you...you are really here." His fingers brushed the hair away from my face.

"Did you lose everything?"

"Some of it is busted up pretty bad, but we'll be fine. I've got it under control. There is nothing broken that cannot be repaired or replaced." He touched my chin.

I closed my eyes as the tears fought to come out. "Cliff, I can't do this!"

"Can't do what, love?"

"I can't be without you." He took a step back and looked at me right in the eyes.

"Are you saying what I think you are saying?" He was smiling.

"I want to be with you. Now. Always."

"So what's it going take for me to get you to pack up your things and come up to St. Joseph and get married?"

"You asking me is all."

"Della, I have been asking you for the last three months. Are you saying yes to me?"

"I'm saying yes to you."

He grinned. "When?"

"Now. But I need a little time to plan this. I have to pack and...where would we be married?"

"There's a church in St. Joseph. I kind of like it. I'll go on up there, find us a decent place to live for the season, and make arrangements at the church. I'll give you a few weeks to get everything sorted out. Does that work for you?"

"It works a lot better than just having you go there alone."

"You will not regret this, Della. We will have so much fun together."

He wrapped his arms around me and whispered, "You have just made me the happiest fellow in the world." This time I reached up and kissed him and I was not about to let go.

On April 27, 1916, Mr. Clifford A. Priest and Miss Adella Marie Lawton applied for marriage license number 385 issued by the State of Missouri. The wedding event was reported in the Joplin newspaper.

> *A wedding of interest to Joplin people will be that of Miss Marie Lawton, daughter of Mr. and Mrs. M.J. Lawton, No. 715 Joplin Street, and Clifford A Priest of St. Joseph, Mo. Mr. Priest is more widely known here as Clifford A. Hastings as he played with the Van Dyke-Eaton Stock Company at the Club theatre all winter. The wedding will take place at 1 o'clock Sunday afternoon in the Episcopal Church in St. Joseph. Mr. and Mrs. Lawton, Miss Lawton, and Miss Olive Crockett will leave tonight for Kansas City, where they will visit for a day before going to St. Joseph. Miss Lawton is well-known here and has many friends. She was one of the original members of the Girls Charity Workers. She is an accomplished musician. The young couple will make their home in St. Joseph for the present. The VanDyke Eaton Company will fill a summer engagement there.*

On Sunday, April 30, 1916, this announcement appeared in the Joplin newspaper:

Lawton-Priest

The marriage of Miss Marie Lawton to Clifford A. Priest takes place today in St. Joseph Missouri, in the Episcopalian Church there. This is a happy result of a pretty romance begun several months ago. The bride is the only child of Mr. and Mrs. Mike Lawton, 715 Joplin Street, and among the oldest families here. She is a charter member of the Girl's Charity Workers and also a member of the Episcopalian Church choir. A pretty feature of the wedding will be the long distance music when the choir here will sing a wedding hymn at the appointed hour. The bride will wear a dainty frock of grey crepe de chine with shoes of same shade. Her bonnet is in grey with velvet streamers and trimmed in tiny French rosebuds. Mr. Priest is better known in Joplin under the stage name of Clifford A. Hastings. It was while he was here in stock company this winter at the Club Theatre that the couple met. The bride was at that time employed as a pianist at the theatre. She is an attractive young woman and is widely known here. The couple will reside in St. Joseph for the present where Mr. Priest is in stock. They will return to Joplin next fall with the return of his company to the Club. Mr. and Mrs. Lawton and Miss Olive Crockett were the only persons attending the wedding.

Dedication

This book is based upon the lives of Clifford Hastings and Adella Marie Lawton, my grandparents. The story came to me from the pages of their scrapbook, which is now over one hundred years old. While most of the book is a work of fiction, the theatrical productions are real, along with many of the actors, the places, and the events. The newspaper articles are mostly verbatim, but the author and the publisher of those tattered pages are unknown. Cliff and Adella loved the theater arts, and in their honor, I dedicate this story to the thousands of traveling theatrical performers who entertained America in the late nineteenth and early twentieth centuries. Some of them are characters in this book, playing a fictionalized version of themselves. Many of them did not achieve the notoriety of working in moving pictures and are virtually unknown today, but their significant contribution to early American entertainment should never be forgotten.

Moving pictures, radio, and ultimately television brought an end to the popularity of the traveling companies.

Between 1900 and 1910 approximately three hundred productions, on average, toured the country each year. Most of them originated from shows that had premiered in New York City. By the 1920s the number of touring Broadway plays had dipped to approximately sixty-five shows annually. And in the 1930s, on average, the number settled at about twenty to twenty-five shows annually. These numbers do not measure the vaudeville, burlesque and cheap melodrama circuits, but the same quick reduction hit them as well. By the 1920s the number of specialty acts dropped rapidly, and by the 1930s most of the various touring networks had collapsed.[1]

---

1. Postlewaite, Thomas, *The Cambridge History of American Theatre*, Vol. II (New York: Cambridge University Press, 1999), pp 164–65.

50110802R00147

Made in the USA
Charleston, SC
15 December 2015